CONRI

VALLEY OF WOLVES BOOK 1

KATHI S. BARTON

This is a work of fiction. Names, characters, places, and incidents are products of the author's imagination or are used fictitiously and are not to be construed as real. Any resemblance to actual events, locations, organizations, or persons, living or dead, is entirely coincidental.

World Castle Publishing, LLC
Pensacola, Florida
Copyright © 2025 Kathi S. Barton
Hardback ISBN: 9798285794769
Paperback ISBN: 9798891264120
eBook ISBN: 9798891264137
First Edition World Castle Publishing, LLC, June 2, 2025
http://www.worldcastlepublishing.com
Cover: Cover Designs by Karen
Editor: Karen Fuller

Chapter 1

Conri watched the greenhouse going up. It was larger than he thought it would have been. But then, he knew very little about the management of greenhouses and how many people it would take to run it. His dearest and best friend, Brewster, told him it would require fifty people to handle the daily tasks and ten more to manage the registers and sales floor. His pack was going to benefit the most from the employment of his people working there.

Moving across the valley where his pack was, Conri, as his wolf, stretched out and let his muscles stretch as well. It was a good feeling being a wolf when he'd been a human for nearly four months without a shift to his other self. He was going to enjoy this as much as he could today because he didn't know what tomorrow would bring.

"You're needed at the bank." Growling low, he asked his brother Yanick what the issue was. *"The new banker is asking if people opening new accounts are shifters or not. Then, he turns them away when they answer truthfully. It's not going to be easy for them to cash their*

new checks if he's going to stop them from getting money against the checks that they've been waiting for. He needs to be taken to task."

"He needs to be taken to the woods and killed." Thankfully, his brother didn't agree with him. *"Call Brewster and see what he can do. I believe he has an interest in the bank as well. Something about him owning the land, I believe. While I have you, could you please check on the men and women at the car dealership? I know they were having some issues as well with being paid their full commissions."*

So far, the new businesses coming to town have only made it more difficult for him. Not only was it difficult to get checks cashed, but they were either not receiving all their pay or not receiving any pay at all. Having an income didn't do them any good if they weren't able to spread a bit of their hard-earned cash around. Then he heard from his vampire friend Brewster.

"Yanick just contacted me about the bank. I'm not going there, but my lovely wife is. She'll get it straightened out in no time. Or we'll need to start having a graveyard for people that have pissed her off. You know how she can be." He told Brew that he was afraid of Calla, and with good reason. *"Yes, I'd not say this to her myself, but she's been testing herself out on some of the magic I've given her. Who would have thought that a tiny little human like her would come to mean so much to both of us?"*

"I'm betting by the end of the day, not only will my people get their checks cashed, but we'll need to be learning the name of the new banker. Your mate does not suffer fools lightly, does she?" They both laughed. "All I wanted to do today was let my wolf have a bit of fun. I've been bombarded with one thing after another since I left the pack house."

"I would tell you to ignore all the requests for help, but you'd not do that anymore than I would. You've made yourself indispensable. And part of being a great leader makes it so you have no time for yourself. Sometimes that's good, but like now, I'm betting you wish you could chuck it all and become just another wolf in a pack." Conri agreed with him. "I know you so well, my friend. The bank manager will be dealt with even if I have to step in. What else may I do for you?"

He told him about the dealership and the lack of getting all commissions. "But I can take care of that, I think. It might be a simple thing that they're not getting them put on the checks like they think. I don't know. I'm going to give them the benefit of the doubt or assume they misunderstood something. I don't want to jump to conclusions about something I know very little about."

"Rette is running the daily operations of the place without the benefit of selling cars. He wanted to make things good for those that work for him. If you need me to, I can set up a meeting among the three of us so I can understand how it works as well. Like you, I have people working there too."

He said he sent his brother over there, and if he didn't have any luck, then a meeting would be great. *"Very good. I'll look forward to hearing about it from you. How are things going for you otherwise? Has your mother been keeping you fat and lazy?"*

"You know my mother well enough to know that she's not cooking for anyone including herself anymore. It's really hit or miss if I can get in touch with her. Did I tell you my cousin met his mate? Now, that's all my mom can talk about. How she'll be a great aunt and not even a grandma yet. It's hell being this old with no one to placate your relatives with a mate and babies."

"Everyone coming around is having babies, it seems. I guess progress makes people horney or something. Most of the people in town are having one, I swear to you." Again, they both laughed about other people. *"I must go and see if my mate needs me. She does that less and less of late. Do you suppose she's grown bored living with a vampire?"*

"Doubtful. Calla is a good person. And hellishly right all the time. Did you hear about my books she did for me? Found out I was paying taxes on the land around here that I don't even own. While we struck a deal long ago about my pack being on your land, I know for a fact that I'm not to pay taxes on someone else's land. And that being said, I do wish you'd allow me to pay you something for it."

"No, I have it well in hand. As I told Calla once. I could remodel all the houses in town twice over, and it

wouldn't put a dent in what I have in the way of money. You're a good friend, Conri, and I'd not have money issues coming between us." Conri thanked him. *"Now, I shall go and check on the poor banker. I'm betting that he's regretting getting out of bed this morning if I know my Calla Lily."*

Conri answered questions when they were put to him, but for the rest of the afternoon and well into the evening, he enjoyed being his other half. Being able to run in the woods had always been a particularly good time for him. He also swam in the lake that separated the pack land from Brew's land.

It was all Brew's land, but he'd plotted out enough to allow the wolves free reign around his when they wanted. He would repay him at times by watching over his home and land as well. He'd recently done that when Calla's uncle was trying to kill her because he thought that her money was his to use as he wanted. Daniel didn't last long after he got out of jail. And the best part was no one would ever find his body or be able to test anything for DNA. They'd done such a good job of cleaning up after he was killed.

Conri was just getting into his home when he heard from Brew again. Calla had dealt with the banker, and they'd have no more issues with getting accounts opened up. He'd even gotten the commissions taken care of.

It had been a corporate thing in that the loans for

the cars they sold had to wait ten days before they got it on their checks. It was in the contract the employees had to sign when they sold a car. So if, in a relatively low occurrence, they returned the car within the first few days, the commission wouldn't be paid.

"Thank you for that." Brew also told him that there was a new banker in the bank as well. *"She didn't kill him, did she? Christ, that's all we need, your mate in prison for killing a stupid banker."*

"No, she made a couple of phone calls and got him fired. He wasn't too keen on that either, by the way. So, if you're out and about, keep an eye on her. I will kill him if he so much as looks in her direction." Conri said he'd do that easily. *"Thank you so much, my friend. Now, when the greenhouse is open to the public, hopefully, nothing goes on there it would be a great day."*

After setting up a time to meet in the coming week, Conri took a long hot shower and went to bed. He was in the habit of sleeping in the nude, and tonight was no different. Having worn himself out today, he knew that he'd sleep well. As soon as his head hit the pillow, he was out.

At half past six the next morning, he was up and having breakfast with his mom. The pack provided him with a cook, so it wasn't unusual that she'd come and have the first meal of the day with him. Sometimes, his brothers would join them, but today, it was just the two of them. She told him he looked rested.

"I feel like I got a good night's sleep too. Running around all day yesterday ignoring everything, for the most part, really wore me out. I might have to do that more often." She asked him about the pack meetings. "They're going to start back up now that it's getting to be winter. With summer and kids being off from school, it's been difficult for us to have them then. But I believe everyone is excited for them to start back up."

"You can count on me to do the organizing of food, you know. I won't cook anything, but I can organize the hell out of it." She smiled at him. "You do know if you had a mate, she'd be doing this so I can enjoy my golden years with a newborn cub in my arms."

"Mom, if it were possible, I'd knock up several humans just so you can have what you want. However, I'm not sure anyone is out there for me anymore. I had my chance at happiness, but Dad...well, you know what he did." She looked away from him, but not before he could see the tears that she was shedding. "Carol was a good mate, and I loved her. I'm not sure that I could love like that again."

"She's out there. I know it." He nodded. They'd been having this same conversation for the last fifty years or so. "All right then, I'm going to start bothering your brothers then. Kendrick is next oldest and far too old to be running around flirting with every woman he sees."

"He's a charmer, he is. I believe he could charm his way out of just about everything he gets into and not have any trouble." He thought of his other brothers. All five of them were charmers when it came to women. "Maybe I need to hang out with them more. They seem to have no trouble wooing a woman to their beds."

"Go on with you now. What a thing to tell your mother." She stood up, and so did he. Getting a tight hug from her and a kiss on the cheek, she left him to his day. It was going to be a good day, he hoped and left his house just as the clock chimed the eight o'clock hour.

Conri thought about his mate. Carol hadn't really been good at anything but causing trouble with him and his pack. He'd never told anyone about what really got her killed but for Brew. And only because he'd walked up on him when he was putting a gun in his mouth. It had been just too much for him when she'd been killed with his father.

Now, there was a bastard. His father had caused so much trouble in the pack that even his brothers were considering leaving for another group. The day that he'd been killed by the pack, including him and his brothers were in on it, had been a great day for everyone. Then, not a week later, his wife had committed one of the worst laws by selling images of herself changing from human to wolf and profiting off it. Needless to say, when she was dealt with, he thought that the world was coming down on his head.

He'd also found out that Carol and his father had been stealing from the pack funds that his dad had been in charge of and buying themselves a big house out in California. Why there? He had no idea, but the fact that he found out more and more about them over the next few decades just went to show him how blinded by love he'd been. It had also soured him on finding anyone to mate with since then.

He would play the game about finding himself a mate with his mom as she had no idea what secrets he'd been hiding. Not even his brothers knew of all the things that he'd found out. But he wasn't going to look for a mate again. One had been more than enough for him.

The first thing he did was go over his appointments for the day. He had two this morning and nothing for the rest of the day. Not that people wouldn't be coming in and out of his office all day, including during the times someone had actually made an appointment, but he felt in a better frame of mind to deal with it.

After lunch, he decided to go to town and see

about the new banker. He had no idea how long the man would be in his offices since he was new, but he did want to go and get the lay of the land, so to speak.

The man wasn't in his office like he thought that he'd be. Instead, he was sitting at a makeshift desk, signing up his people for checking accounts for their new paychecks. He liked a man who got down and dirty with his employees, and when talking to Mr. Roger Hamlin, he decided that they couldn't have done better with getting someone to take over for the other man. Hamlin was a wolf shifter and a part of his pack as of the moment they got a moment to sit down and talk.

"I should have come to you sooner, but I wanted to get this taken care of. But I would enjoy being a part of your pack. My other pack leader isn't thrilled that I've come here, but he'll get over it. My boss from the bank was none too happy to get the call from Calla Smith yesterday." He smiled a little. "She was none too happy to be making the call either, but we don't do that to prospective accounts. Banks need all the new accounts we can get."

~*~

Yuri watched as the line behind him got longer and longer. He'd only stopped by the grocery store to pick up some milk and eggs. Had he known some crazy couponer was in the store, he'd have gone someplace else. As it was now, he had a lot of things to do tonight, and one of them wasn't standing in line with a couponer person.

He knew that coupons saved money for those who used them. He'd been guilty of that, too, by holding up the line because his coupon hadn't worked the way he had thought that it should. But this woman had hundreds of them. And the way she was watching the cashier, he knew she was wanting to get every one of them to work.

"She's scanning them too quickly." He might not have heard the woman behind him if he didn't have special hearing because he was a wolf. But she might be right. Watching the cashier scan the coupons, it looked like she was having a race with herself to get them scanned. "The system will shut down if you keep this up, Milly."

Intrigued, he turned to look at the woman. Christ, he nearly swallowed his tongue. She was that beautiful. Instead of saying something stupid, he asked her what would happen if she did shut the system down. She eyed him with a cocked brow.

"I didn't say anything." He nodded and said that she had, and he would like to know if he had to get his milk and eggs elsewhere. "I'd say yes. If the system shuts down, then neither register will work, and they'll have to void all of her purchases and redo her order. And I didn't speak out loud. You must have heard me whispering."

"I did." He looked at the couponer and then at the cashier. "She's going to fuck it up for all of us, isn't she?"

"I'd say that's about right. Milly thinks that if she beats the computer on the register—has the coupons still ringing up when she's finished with them, she gets herself a mental prize. Only she knows what that will be. But she's done this before." She eyed him hard. "What are you? Wolf, I'm thinking."

"You'd be correct." He turned back to her, winked, and then smiled. "My name is Yuri Valley. I'm with the local pack that's around here."

"Good for you. I'm Cassidy Warmer. I work here a few days a week. I also work at the Warmer Horse Farm too. Yes, I'm related, but I don't have any money, so save your flirting for someone else. My sister, perhaps." He couldn't help it, he laughed. Then he asked if she was as pretty as she was. "Cynthia is gorgeous. She tells me that all the time."

Again, he couldn't help himself. He laughed. She was delightful and funny. And he had no doubt that Cassidy was much more beautiful than her sister was and twice as engaging. He was just about to ask her out when she groaned.

"Cassidy, can you be a sweetheart and open

another line for me? Milly has her hands full." Instead of answering him, she told him about the coupons and explained how Milly was going to shut down the computer. The man, he assumed the store manager, came out of the little cubby hole he was in and put his hand on the scanner. "Milly, if this shuts down again, I'm going to fire you. I've had enough of your shenanigans. Stand there until the computer has time to catch up."

She did, but she wasn't the least bit ashamed of her actions. Instead, she popped her gum loudly and glared at Cassidy. The manager asked her again if she'd open up a register for him.

"It's my day off." He said he'd pay her double. "Whatever. Just bring me out a clean drawer, and I'll take the customers in line right now. Then I'm going home. I have a life other than this, you know."

"I know, sweetie, but Milly didn't tell me that Mrs. Craine was coming in today. I would have scheduled you to take the order. You get her in and out quickly." Mrs. Craine said she didn't bitch as much, either. "There is that. All right, everyone, just go to the other line, and Cassidy will get you all out of here lickty split."

In less time than it took her to count out her drawer, he was on his way home. But he didn't want to go and had even thought about staying in Milly's line so that he could linger around more. Taking his purchases to his car, he decided to go back in and ask Cassidy out. He felt like they'd had a personal connection. But by the time he was back in the store, she had gotten the other customers out of her line and was in the cubby hole with the manager. He didn't want to interrupt her, so he waited until she was finished before smiling at her at the door.

"What do you want?" He laughed. He'd laughed more today than he had in a few weeks. He asked her to go to dinner with him. "Are you addled? I said my sister was way prettier. Not to mention better at dates than I'd ever be. I'll even give you her phone number."

"How about you give me yours instead?" She blew her bangs off her face, and he wanted to see if it was as soft as it looked. There was something about this prickly little thing that had him wanting to take her out and pamper her. And he had no idea where that thought had come from. "I'd very much like to take you out to dinner. What harm can come from that?"

"You have no idea. All right. I'll give you my number and my sisters. I'm sure that once you think about it, you'll come to the conclusion that I'm not proper date material. I blow my nose at the table, and my mother thinks that I have no idea which fork to use. Why would you need so many forks for one meal?

Anyway." She pulled out a small paper bag and wrote down her number in small numbers and her sisters in large ones. He was still laughing when she left him there with his paper bag.

By the time he was home, he was smiling. Making reservations at his favorite restaurant that had about anything you could want on the menu, he picked up his cell to call Cassidy. He should have known she'd not give in that easily when he got Cynthia on the line. She asked him who he was.

"Yuri Valley. And I'm trying to find your sister, Cassidy. I had made plans with her to go to dinner." She said that her sister didn't live in the big house but she'd go out with him. "I'm sorry, I don't know you. I was really hoping to get Cassidy."

"Oh, you can get to know me over dinner. You can pick me up at the big house, that's where I live with mommy and Daddy. Cass, as I said, doesn't live here anymore. Is six all right with you?" He was stuck, and he had a feeling that Cassidy had done this before and gotten away with it. He told Cynthia that he'd call her and see if they were still on tonight. "Oh, don't bother her. She never dates. That's why we don't get along all that well. She is a fuddy-duddy. And not nearly as pretty as I am."

There it was, the, she told me that she's prettier than I am, quote. Getting off the phone with Cynthia was harder than he thought it would be, but she was wearing him down. Instead of giving in to her whiney attempts to get him to go out with her, he told her that he had to go. He had things to do.

"I'll see you at six on the dot. Don't be late. Also, I need to know what sort of dress to wear too. Will this be a fancy dinner or just a regular meal? I mean, how many people will be there to see me?" Yuri asked her if she cared what he looked like. "I'm assuming that you're related to the Valley family around here. I've seen most of you running around. All of you are hunky men that I don't mind being with."

Christ, she was a piece of work. "I'm not going to be picking you up, Cynthia. I'm looking for your sister. It's been nice talking to you, but I have to go."

"I'll see you at six on the dot then." Yuri closed the connection. He didn't want any trouble with this woman or her family, but he'd not called her to have a date. Picking up the phone again, he called the store that he'd met her in. It was a long shot, but he was going to see if he could get in touch with Cassidy that way.

"Oh, she's here right now. Came in to pick up the things that she'd had in her hands when I asked her to work." He asked if he could talk to her. "Sure, sure. I'll go get her. Hang on, young man."

It wasn't as long as a wait that he'd thought it

would be. As soon as she said her name, he told her that her sister was expecting him to pick her up at six. Then he told her what kind of things she'd said to him.

"She's really good at getting what she wants. If you have money, which I'm assuming you do, then she'll be on you like white on rice. Cynthia has long claws, and they're dangerous." He said that she owed him. "Owe you what? I told you that I didn't want to date. How is that my fault...Well, I guess it's my fault that Cynthia caught you off guard. I tell you what. I'll go out to the big house, and you can pick which one of us you want to...no, that won't work either. She'll take one look at your truck and be all pissy about you not having a limo or something. I'll just meet you at the house for dinner. I have to go there anyway, and you might as well suffer the way I do. All right?"

"I'm having dinner with you and your family then." She told him that if he had to have dinner with her, it had to be there because she'd been summoned home. "Summoned? They really do that?"

"You have no idea the links they'll go to reign me into their world." She was hurting, and he could tell. "Do you still want to date me? I mean, after this one time, you'll see why I never date."

"Yes, even if I have to have dinner with your family, I want to see you." She told him to dress in a suit and tie then, and she'd be in a dress. "What's happening at this dinner? Should I have a heads up?"

"I honestly have no idea. I've been summoned, as I said, and once I get there, I'll be told. We should have exchanged blood or something. That way, I could tell you to run to the hills if necessary." He said that they could still do that. "All right. I don't know you all that well, but I would like to keep you from harm. They can do what they want to me, but I'd hate for you to get caught up in things. Cynthia has been ordered to stay for dinner, too, so that gets you off the hook with her." Yuri started to tell her that he wasn't planning on dating her anyway when Cassidy spoke again. "I'm sorry I got you into this. You can change your mind if you want. There will be no hard feelings, I promise."

"I'll be there. And we'll exchange blood so that I can cheer you on if you need it." She laughed like it had surprised her somewhat. "There you go. It'll be fine. I'll be there at six with my best foot forward. All right?"

"Yes, all right. But don't say I didn't warn you." He wasn't worried that she had tried to talk him out of coming. He was more worried about her. And in that moment, he realized something else. He wanted to protect her with all that he was. And he also knew she wasn't his mate, so he was confused about that.

Going to his closet, he was glad that he'd just got his suit out and had it cleaned. It was black with silver pinstripes that he wore when he had a meeting with someone. Finding a tie that he loved that was sort of neutral, he decided to polish his shoes as well. Then he thought about his boots and took them off to be cleaned up. Yes, he thought, he was going to make an impression if it was the last thing he did.

Conri came over just as he was trying to get his tie on right. Taking over for him, Conri had him fixed up in just a few minutes. Then he asked him where he was going. After telling him the entire story about how he'd been tricked and was now going to go to dinner with her family, Conri asked him if he was sure that he wanted to do that.

"I do. I don't know why, but I do want to see what they have plans for her. I've been thinking about her since I got out of the shower, and I've come to the conclusion that I don't want to date her so much as I want to protect her. Isn't that weird?" His brother said that it was. "Thanks. I can always count on you to bring me back to earth, can't I?"

"If you need me or any of us, let me know. I'll be ready to come and get you if you need me. Something about this whole thing makes me a bit nervous for you." He thanked him again. "I'll be on standby for you. Just don't...I don't know. Don't get married or rooked into getting married while you're out there."

Now, he had something else to worry about.

Not getting married, he knew they couldn't do that to him, but what else could be going on with this family? He wished now he'd taken the option of bailing out. He might well have saved himself some headache.

Chapter 2

Cassidy watched the drive for Yuri. When she saw his big truck pulling into the driveway of the house, she went out on the front porch to greet him. Really, she was going to give him one more chance to get away, but almost as soon as he touched her, he took her hand to his mouth and bit down on it. The connection was instantaneous.

"Well, hello there. But I don't like the truck. Next time, you come for me in a nice car." Cynthia came out on the front porch as well. "See? Didn't I tell you that I was prettier than Cass? She has such a manly body."

"I think she's just perfect. And while you are pretty, Cass has a natural beauty that makes her shine. I even love her freckles." Cynthia told him he wasn't getting on her good side. "As I told you several times when we were talking, I'm here to see Cass. She and I had plans for tonight."

"*You're going to piss her off. It's not a pretty site when she doesn't get her way. I love it.*" Yuri smiled at her and took her hand into his. She let him, too. This was just too much fun not to have a little at the expense of her sister. *"I still don't know why we're here, but I'll let you know when I find out."*

"Good. Does she really tell everyone that she's prettier than you are?" She only told him *yes* and led him into the stately home. *"This isn't going to be fun, is it?"*

"It's never fun when I get summoned home." She smiled at him, and he could almost taste the pain on her face. "Yuri, I'd like for you to meet my father, Howard Warmer, and my mother, Elizabeth. You've already spoken to Cynthia. My older brother Howie is running late, and he'll be here by the time dinner is ready to be served." Yuri shook hands with both her parents and said hello to Cynthia.

"Daddy, Yuri was supposed to be my date tonight. Not Cass'. What am I going to do without a man on my arm, and she has one? It's not fair." Her father ignored Cynthia in favor of talking to Yuri. Then she turned to her. "You think you're so smart. I could get him if I wanted him."

"Okay." She and her sister used to be really close when they were children. Then Cynthia found boys, and she'd been in competition with her since. Not that Cassidy ever played the games that her sister did with boys and now men. She didn't live here, so she could go out with whomever she wanted, and her sister never knew. "He's a friend of mine, and that's all. We might go out some more if he asks, but there really isn't anything between us."

"Well, I'm putting my foot down. You're not allowed to date anyone until I approve them." Cassidy asked her if she was serious. "Yes. When it comes to men, I'm always serious. Once you see someone, you'll tell me their name so I can look them up and see if they're worthy of dating me. If he is, you'll back off and try again. I won't be fooled by this little sister. Or I'll tell daddy on you."

"Tell him what? That you're laying down the law to keep me from finding someone to go out with? What's this really about?" She told her. "Sloppy seconds? But isn't that what you're doing to me? I can't date until you don't want them anymore? I'll date whoever I want whenever I want, and there isn't shit you can do about it."

"Cassidy Warmer. Watch your language in my home." She looked at her dad, and she could see a hint of humor on his face. "Cynthia, you'll behave yourself, or I'll turn what you just said around so that Cassidy gets what she wants."

"That's not fair. She always gets what she wants, Daddy." She started for the stairs to no doubt slam her bedroom door. But father told her she was going to have dinner with them all even if he had to beat her ass—double standard there on cursing, she thought—to get her back down here on time. "Mommy, make them do what I want."

"I have a headache, Cynthia. I don't know what is going on, but I want nothing to do with it. Howard, our son is here. Let's go into the dining room where I can have a seat." Mother usually gave in to her sister and made her do whatever she wanted. But today, with this argument, she had won. But it wouldn't last long, she knew, and she was going to take what joy she got out of Cynthia being upset with both parents. "Come along now. Bring your young man through, too, Cassidy. We'll have a lovely meal, then your father can have a word with all of you."

Yuri was seated next to her. As he pulled her chair out, she watched as Cynthia struggled to get someone to do the same for her. Finally, she got Howie to do it.

"I can tell you why you're all here if you want to know." She asked Yuri if it was bad. *"Yes. Your father has a tumor on his brain that isn't operatable. He's known about it for a week now, and he needs to start on chemotherapy."* Yuri took her hand under the table and squeezed it. *"I'm so very sorry, Cass. He's going to talk to you all about getting settled before he leaves this world."*

"You're joking? He wants us to get married and have a home life before he — how long does he have?" Yuri told her that he'd been given a year, but he didn't think he was going to make it that long.

"*It's a good-sized tumor. They did a biopsy on it a week ago.*" She didn't want anything to happen to her dad. Or her mom, for that matter. It wasn't until Yuri squeezed her hand again that she started paying attention at the table.

The meal was a blur. When someone would ask her something, Yuri would squeeze her hand, and she'd pay attention enough to speak, but then she'd go right back to being upset. It wasn't until her dad stood up that she put all her focus on him.

"I have an inoperable tumor on my brain. I have less than a year to live." And just like that, he left them to go to the living room. As soon as Cynthia started wailing that her poor daddy was going to die, she got up and went to the living room with her father. The only other person that came into the room with her was Yuri. She asked him why he'd told them like he had. "I needed to let you know all at one time, and this seemed to be the best possible way. Having your young man here, it gave me strength. I don't know why, but he did. So, I guess thank you for that."

"So that's it? You told us you were going to die in a year and think that what? We'd be all right with that? I have news for you, Buster, I'm not all right with that. We might not have seen eye to eye on a great many things, but you're still my father, and I'm not going to allow you to die without getting some answers." He looked at her with tears in his eyes. "Dad, don't do that. I'm not going to wail at you like Cynthia did, but I'm going to get all slobby with my heart breaking if you cry, too."

"I'm going to miss you most of all, I think." She looked in the doorway when he did and was glad that it was empty. "You've been...well, Cassidy, you've been the one that keeps me laughing and going for all these years. I don't want to leave you."

"Oh, Dad, don't say that. I'm here if you need me." He told her that he did need her here with him in his final year. "You want me to move back in? Dad, that's not a good thing. You remember why I was asked to leave."

"I was a fool for giving into her demands. I want you here with me. I need someone to distract me when I'm having a pity party for myself. Play some chess with me when I'm in need of a little competition." He reached out for her hand, and she gave it to him. "Please say that you'll move back in here and keep me company. Please, my child."

"All right. I'll do it." She turned and looked at Yuri. "I'm sorry about all this. I'm glad that you're here. Would you take me for a ride someplace? Anyplace?"

After telling her dad that she'd be back later, he hugged and kissed her on the cheek. Then, when her mother joined them in the living room, she told her that she was going out and would return later. Nodding once, she asked if Dad had asked her yet. With a nod, she was out the door and in the big truck that all the Valley men had when they were out and about.

She didn't know how long they'd been driving when she realized they were in front of the Dari Q. Still upset, she wasn't sure she could eat anything when Yuri said he was getting her a shake. She told him she needed a chocolate malt with chocolate ice cream. He kissed her on the cheek and got out of his truck. She was really hungry all of a sudden and couldn't wait for him to return.

When he brought her the malt, she sat in his warm truck and drank it. He was waiting on more food and wondered why he'd not gotten enough to eat at her house. Then she remembered that he was a wolf, and it more than likely wasn't enough for him, whatever it had been. For the life of her, she couldn't remember one thing about the meal she'd had with her family.

Getting into the truck, he handed her a foil-wrapped something. Opening it up, she was thrilled that he'd got her a burger, too. The four that he had on his lap made her laugh. It felt good to be around him when he could make her laugh with what she'd gone through at home.

"I'm sorry about tonight. And it would serve

me right if you never wanted to see me again." He finished one of the burgers and looked at her. She told him again how sorry she was. "I should have known it wasn't going to be good because it never is at our family dinners."

"I've been talking to my mom." She nodded and shoved the last bite of burger in her mouth, reaching for another one. She didn't feel bad when he said they were for himself. Then he gave her one of them. "You seem to know a great deal about shifters. So I'm assuming that you know what a mate is?"

"Yes. I used to work with a couple of wolves. I believe they were a part of your pack. Anyway, I also worked with other shifters, and they all have mates or hope they do. Why did you contact your mother?" He ate another burger while she was just getting the foil off her second one. "You'd better go and order some more now so they'll be ready when you are."

He told her that was a good idea and got out of the truck, leaving just one of the burgers left behind. When he returned, saying they were going to bring them out to him, he turned and looked at her while he polished off the last of his stash.

"I told my mom how I felt about you." She asked if she was his mate. "No. I wish you were, but you're not. However, I do have feelings for you. I have this overwhelming need to protect you like my sister or something along those lines. Mom seems to think that these feelings are here because you are my sister and mate to one of my brothers. I'll be back. I forgot to order myself a drink."

She was glad that she'd eaten before he dropped that bombshell on her. Putting the last bite back in the foil, she thought about what he was saying. His brother's mate. While he didn't say who, she didn't know any of them like she did Yuri, and that wasn't saying a great deal. She barely knew him. When he got back in the truck, she asked him how many brothers he had.

"Five and a sister. But she's found her mate a long time ago and rarely comes around anymore." She waited until he finished eating before asking him about his brothers. Honestly, she didn't know what to ask him. But she did want to know if any of them were pricks like her brother could be. "Nah. Conri is the alpha to our back of about four hundred wolves. Since he's the alpha, if you're his mate, you'd be his alpha bitch. Not in a bad way. It's just what they call her. Then there is Kendrick. He's a doctor right now. Nice guy if you ask me. Yanick is funny like you are. I'm hoping that you're mated to him. You'll enjoy his sense of humor. He's a cook at one of the restaurants in Columbus. But he doesn't like it anymore, so he will change to something else soon. Rette and Lamar are twins, but they look nothing alike. Rette is more of Mom's coloring, and Lamar is darker like Dad was. They're both artists. Then there is me. I keep us all in money by investing what we have because we've been around a long time."

"How long have you been around? I'm assuming here that you're a good deal older than you look." He nodded and asked her if she freaked out. "Not normally, no. You might say I'm sort of jaded about life in general. How old?"

"Conri is the oldest and has been around about four hundred years. I'm the youngest, and I'm still nearly three hundred and fifty years old." She nodded and felt her belly churn up a bit. "Are you going to be sick?"

"No. I don't believe so. But that is a lot to take in." He told her he was sorry. "I'll be all right. I'm just calculating how much older you guys are than me. I'm only twenty-four."

~*~

Conri was the last of his brothers to go and see Cassidy. She was working today at the grocery store and seemed to be really busy. She'd looked up at him several times since he came into the store on the ruse to buy bread. Finally, when she was finished with the customer in front of him, she spoke.

"You here to sniff around? As you can see, I'm

busy and don't have time for your crap. Get it over with so that I can go home and be assured that I'm not going to have to bow down before some jerk that only comes in the store for—do you even need that loaf of bread?" He shook his head, too stunned by her anger toward him. "Well, you'd better put it back where you got it from before you leave here. I don't have time to front and face the store after you're gone. Get it over with."

He hadn't any idea what front and face the store meant, but he turned to take the bread back like she'd told him. Before he was even halfway there, she called him back to get his 'sniffing' over with for her. Inhaling deeply, he knew in that moment what he'd been fearing for the last couple of weeks. She was his mate.

"I'll put the bread back. You're my mate." He took the bread back to the aisle and hoped that he put it where it belonged. He was so blinded by uncertainty. Instead of talking to the woman again, she was busy with the next customer, he left the store and headed to his truck. Sitting in it, he sat there thinking about what all this meant and what it would mean for his future.

Leaving the lot, he was nearly home when his mom contacted him. She asked if he was still in town and, if so, if would he pick up a gallon of ice cream for her. She wanted a banana split. Telling her that he was nearly home, a fat lie, he said to send one of the others to get it for her. She asked him what was wrong. Before he could think about what it might mean to tell her what he'd just discovered, he blurted it out to her that he'd found his mate.

"You're joking. If you are, I don't think this is the least bit funny, Conri. I don't want to have my hopes dashed when you tell me it's not true." He told her it was true that the little human at the grocery store was his mate. *"Then Yuri was right in thinking that he needed to protect her."*

"From me?" Mom didn't answer him, but he could almost taste her anger. *"I meant nothing by that, Mom. I'm still reeling from the fact that she's there and a human. I only just found out. Cut me some slack for a few moments."*

"What did you say to her? I'm sure that it was a coming together like none other." He told her what had happened and what he'd said to her. *"You didn't just tell her that and walk away, Conri. Please tell me that you were more polite than that. I'd like to think I raised you better than that."*

"She asked me if I was there sniffing around. Sniffing around like she was a piece of prime meat, and I was there to check her out." Mom asked him why he'd gone there in the first place if it wasn't to sniff her out. *"Like you said, I was raised better than that. But now that I think about it,*

I suppose she was correct. All of us have been there under one ruse or another to see if she was our mate. I should have gone first, then she might not have been so upset with me. I'll make it up to her. I'll try and be nice when I go get her to talk to her."

"*Talk to her or at her? You know that there is a difference."* His mom sighed heavily, and again, he could taste her emotion. This time, it was disappointment. *"Just be nice to her, Conri. This is all new to her as well. You have to realize that, don't you?"*

He found himself in the store parking lot again. This time, he was parked far enough away from the glass front so she wouldn't be able to see him. Sniffing around, indeed. He'd come there with high hopes that his brother was wrong. He didn't want another mate. Carol had been more than enough for him.

Conri thought about his first mate. It had been so long ago now that he could barely remember her face. And if not for the tintypes that he had of the two of them together, he might well have forgotten her long ago. But he'd never forget her betrayal, the way that she'd got with his father and robbed him of everything he could have hoped for in having a mate. Not to mention the pack that they'd taken money from. Thousands of dollars had been stolen from the pack and his family for them to get together after robbing them of everything they could put their hands on. And two hundred years hadn't lessened the pain that he felt from thinking about all of it.

The pounding at his window had him jumping a little bit. It was Cassidy, and she looked fiery mad. He rolled down the window, and she shoved a paper bag at him. He was barely able to catch it before it fell in his lap.

"Your mother called. She said that you forgot to get her ice cream. You owe me five bucks. I'm charging you that much because that's what it cost me to bring it out here to you." She started away, and he was still holding the ice cream; the cold treat was freezing his hands. Before he could get his wits about him, she was already across the lot and into the store again. That's when it occurred to him that she was beautiful. Not that he wanted her in his life any more than he did before, but the way she walked, really stomped across the lot, made him smile. Conri was losing his mind.

Going home, he handed the ice cream to his mom and asked her to give him some time. When she tsked at him, she left him in the front hall. Instead of following her to find out what he'd done now, he went to his office and started to work on the projects that he'd left too long without any closure. He really needed to get his head in the game.

When he was brought a cup of tea, his mother sat down across from him. She eyed him hard, and when he realized that both screens had gone dark and that he was no closer to getting anything done than he'd been when he came in here, he asked her what he was supposed to do.

"What do you mean? What are you supposed to do? You have a mate, son. You're supposed to woo her or whatever they call it nowadays when a man finds the woman of his dreams." He said he didn't think she was going to be anything like his dreams had pictured. "This is because of Carol, isn't it? You do know that she's not her, don't you? That she's been dead longer than she'd been alive. Every woman that you meet isn't her, Conri. You have to let the past go."

"I don't know that I can. To be honest with you, I never thought that I'd have to deal with a mate again. They're demanding and—" She told him again that not all women were Carol. "I know that in my head, but my heart doesn't have room for another person to hurt me."

He'd never said that aloud before. He'd known it in his head that was the reason that he didn't pursue women. It was hard for him to not judge other women by the way he'd been treated. Not only did she leave him for his father, but she had done it in such a public way that he'd been humiliated by it as well. And he still kept some of that in his head after all this time.

"I don't know how to help you, son, if you're not

going to be willing to try. Yuri said that she's nice and pretty. Said she's also dealing with a looney family and that her dad just found out that he has a brain tumor that only gives him about a year to live." He said that Yuri said that she's strong-willed, too. "Oh, what does he know? I doubt any woman has ever said no to him. He's too cute and charming to be out on his own. All I can say about any of you is that I'm glad that you're wolves, or I'd have fifty or more grandchildren by who knows how many women."

He laughed as she did. Yes, the way his younger brothers dated and slept around, it was a good thing that they couldn't have kids with any women but with their mates. He himself usually found himself a shifter to…relax with. They understood that there was going to be nothing between them, and that was all it was, just sex. Of course, he didn't tell his mom that. She'd embarrass him in some way.

After having his tea, he set to work. He really did have a lot to do, and he'd been putting things off thinking about having a mate in the woman at the store. It had been two weeks since Yuri had told them all about her, and they had each gone to see her that first few days. He'd been a fool to put it off and was feeling terrible about the way that he'd treated her this morning.

By dinner time, he was just finishing up the last

file. He had five neat stacks of files that would be given to each of his brothers to follow up on. There were also two files that he had to turn back over to Yuri so that he could see what he could do about some investments that he'd been looking into. Yuri was fantastic at keeping them in money and investing in their future. All his brothers had good jobs, too.

He decided to see if he could get in touch with Cassidy and have dinner with her. He'd been thinking about how rude he'd been this morning and wanted to make it up to her. She should be off work by now, and he was going to see if Yuri had a phone number that he could use. He thought that she was living at the ranch where her parents lived but wasn't sure. He'd been told she'd been asked to come back home.

That was something that he needed to be made aware of, too. Why was she living outside of the family home? He had heard about the sister demanding that Cassidy not date anyone until she gave her permission. Conri wondered what she'd say when he wanted nothing to do with her nor her term, "sloppy seconds." Yuri had been slightly pissed about that and how the sister, Cynthia, had tried to get a date with him. That's all he needed was a strange family to deal with.

Yuri not only gave him her cell phone number but also her address where she was living. Yes, she was at the big house, which they called the family home because her father had asked her to move back home.

"There's something really odd going on there, Con. Like, I think the sister is extremely entitled, and the brother strikes me as a lazy fuck." He asked him why he thought that when he came by the office to get the paperwork that he had for him. "Mr. Warmer, Howard said that Cassidy was the only one that he really cared for. And then, when we were leaving, he told her that she was going to be all right living at home again. I have a feeling that the sister and brother aren't all that nice to their sister. And then last night, when she called me, she was upset but tried her best not to show it. Like something was said to her, and it hurt her heart."

"You talk to her a lot?" He told him that she was his friend before she'd become his mate. "I didn't mean anything like that. I'm just wondering how much you know about her that I don't."

"Not much, I'm betting. She's very...I was going to say reserved, but that's not it either. She's very outspoken when she feels she needs to be. Last night, while we were talking—you do know that I have a connection with her, right? Anyway, while we were talking, her sister came to her door and was pounding on it. She told me she was demanding entrance so that she could see what she was doing. Since she wasn't on her phone, she told her that she'd better not be setting anything up with anyone, or she'd find out. I have no idea why, but I have a feeling that she's going to make it really difficult for the two of you to get to know each other." Conri said it would be none of her business. "Maybe not, but that won't stop her. And Cynthia has a one-set mind. She won't take no for an answer either."

When his brother left him, he decided to call her now in order to set up a time for them to get together. He didn't know the family, so he didn't feel the need to clear anything with them. Especially the sister. He'd deal with her, too, if it came to that. Picking up his cell phone, he dialed the number that he had. When she answered, he could tell that something had happened and asked her about it.

"Can I meet you in town? I'm assuming that you're Conri Valley, right?" He said that he was and wanted to take her to dinner. "That would be fantastic. I'll meet you in the parking lot at the store. I'm not dressed for anything fancy, so burgers would be great. I'll see you in ten minutes."

Then she hung up. It would take him that long to get there if he hurried and was out the door before telling anyone where he was headed. If his mom wanted him home, she'd contact him, and he'd tell her what he was doing. Whatever happened to Cassidy, he could tell that she was upset by the way she was tense with her words. He pulled into the lot just as she did.

Before he could put his truck in park, she was coming toward him and got in with him. Whatever was going on, she burst into tears as soon as she was buckled into the seat.

Chapter 3

Cynthia searched the entire house for her sister. The little bitch was dating when she told her that she wasn't to do that until she'd dated them first. And if she thought that she was going to be all right with her running off like she did, then Cynthia was going to show her a thing or two about that as well.

She didn't like that everyone thought that Cass was prettier than her. She didn't see it. Her sister was so plain that she just didn't even think of her as passing nice looking. Cass didn't care if she had freckles all over her face, nor did she ever go and have her hair done up into a nice style. Her sister was just painfully plain. And she didn't like her.

Ever since she'd been fourteen, Cynthia had been the center of attention. She'd gotten her boobs early and didn't have any trouble using them with the boys to get them to like her. Cass had been born about the time she was able to get out on her own at sixteen, and it had been a competition since in getting boys and now men to look at her. Not that Cass cared if they looked at her. No, she was more into playing chess with their father and mucking out stalls around the ranch.

Once, she'd caught her hosing off at the stalls outdoors and had about fifty men watching her. Not really that many, but it seemed like it to her. Cynthia put a stop to that right then and there by going to her daddy and making it so that Cass no longer worked in the stalls. That was the first of many things that she put a stop to concerning her little sister. And now she was flaunting dating in her face.

Looking in the mirror in the front hall, Cynthia could see that she was beginning to look her age. Forty wasn't anything that she could do anything about, but she'd not been married yet, and no suitors were coming to the door anymore just for her. And even though she'd never had a child to term, her body was beginning to look out of shape in places that she didn't care for.

She had saggy upper arms. Her thighs were full of cellulite, and no matter how tight her pants or stockings were, she couldn't hide it from anyone anymore. She also had a floppy neck. Chicken neck, one of her now no longer friends told her. While she was beginning to look like a forty-year-old single woman, her sister was at the prime of her life and didn't seem to be getting anything that she had when she turned twenty-four.

Reduced to calling her, she wasn't surprised that she'd not answered her phone. Pulling out her list of things that she'd done to piss her off today, Cynthia wrote down that she was to answer her phone when she called. It was mandatory for her to be able to speak to her at all times.

"Daddy will take my side on this. Her leaving the house is a big no-no, too. How am I supposed to keep track of her if she's not here?" Mother came into the room she was in, and Cynthia told her to go away. "I'm busy doing things in here, Mother, and you're not helpful with me concerning Cass."

"Why don't you leave her alone, Cynthia? She's a grown woman and knows her own mind. If she wants to date everyone in the county, that's no concern to you." She told her that she didn't understand what her dating could do to her. "Nothing. You wouldn't be dating the men that she does anyway because she's so much younger than you are."

"What a nasty thing to say to me. I'm just as pretty as she is. More so, actually. She won't even put on blush when she goes out. Or lipstick. How do men even find that to be appealing?" Mother asked her who knew the minds of men nowadays. "I do. And she's not going to go out with men that might want to date me instead. I'm the oldest, and if she thinks I'm going to be all right with her taking over my dating pool, then she'd better be careful that I don't ruin that ugly face of hers."

"Cynthia Jane Warmer. What a terrible thing to say about your own flesh and blood. You should be ashamed of yourself." She told her that she wasn't and that if Cass decided to go against her, she'd teach her not to cross her. "I just don't understand you at all anymore. You're one argument away from having a stroke the way that you're acting. You don't want to go back to that home, do you?"

"No, never, and you'd better watch yourself, too, mother. I'm not so sure that you're not going to be on my list of things that I have my daddy take care of for me." She asked her why she thought that her husband would do anything against her. "Because I'll tell him what I want, and he'll do it for me because he loves me more than he does you. You'll see. I'll have you both in trouble if you don't watch it."

Mother left her there without another word. It was just as well; she didn't want her around anymore anyway. Mother was forever telling everyone how old she was, and it was reflecting badly on her to know that her mom was in her sixties. Howie was still in his twenties—he'd just turned twenty-nine a few weeks ago. It was bad enough that her father had this brain tumor thing and was taking all the attention from her anyway. Now, her mother was acting up. She decided to call Howie to find out what he was going to do about Cass dating.

After telling him everything on her list, she asked him which ones she could cross off that he was going to take care of for her. He blustered around for a few minutes, trying like her mother did to figure out why she'd care about what their little sister was doing.

"Because she's annoying me to no end. This whole dating thing has to stop, and you should be upset, too." He asked her why, as if he couldn't figure it out on his own. "You'll see what is going to happen. I'm going to have to take charge of her, just as I should have done when she was born. Mother has let her get by with too much, and now my daddy is going to have to take her on to keep her in line. I have rules. Rules that she's breaking."

"You see, that's where we differ. I don't care who she dates, and it has no effect on me whatsoever. So long as we're not dating the same person, I'm fine with her—" She told him not to be disgusting. "I'm just saying, Cynthia, you should be finding yourself a husband and leave her to her own self. There is nothing to be done about her dating, and I hope she finds someone that treats her right."

"You bastard. Why is it just me who has to do everything? Well, there's no hope for it. I'm going to have to get into her business and make sure that she's not doing anything to harm me. She will, too, just because I told her not to do it." Howie asked her if she was off her meds again. "I don't take those anymore. I'm better without them. Besides, that's nothing to do with Cass. She's behaving badly, and it's reflecting back on me."

"You're insane. Again. I'm going to call Mom and Dad and let them know that you're not taking your meds. You were told not to stop taking them about fifteen years ago when you had that episode. Remember that? They had to lock you into one of those homes." She said that they were wrong to do that to her. "It saved your life, didn't it."

"I was just fine. And I don't know what you're talking about saving my life. I was doing things that needed to be done, and I was getting them done when I was taken to that home." Howie told her that she really did need to get back on her meds. "I'm not going to spend the rest of my life doped up because some quack said I was mentally insane."

"He didn't say that. He never said you were insane. He said you have a chemical imbalance, and when you're on your medications, you do better with everything. You're not thinking well, and that's going to get you into trouble again." She hung up on him. He wasn't making any sense when she was talking about her sister, and he was going on about meds. She didn't need them for the first time in years. She was thinking right.

"He'd better not tell Daddy either. I'll show him how all right I am if he does." She tried to call Cass again and when some man answered. "Who is this, and what have you done with my sister?"

"Nothing. She's having a nice dinner with me." She screamed at him. "You must be the older sister that I've been hearing about. You might as well get used to the idea of the two of us seeing one another. She's my mate."

"I don't care what she thinks she is to you. You'll be dating me first. And if I decide that you're not good enough for me, which I'm thinking right now isn't going to happen. I'll allow her to date you. But just because she's broken the rules, I'm going to marry your ass and see how that goes with her. I'm her boss." He laughed. "What do you find so funny? Nothing that I don't approve of either, I'm assuming."

"Your dad approves, so I'm not worried about you." She asked him what he'd done with her daddy. "He's having dinner with us right now. Never have I seen a man enjoy a shake and French fries like he does. I'm guessing you don't approve of him having a good dinner with me, either. Well, Cindy, you're in for a lot of things not going your way in the future if I have anything to say about it." She screamed again, this time right into the phone.

"You put my daddy on the line right now, you idiot, so that I can have a private conversation with him." He said he'd put it on speaker. "You'll do as I tell you, or so help me, I'll ruin your fat face. Then who would date you? No one, including my sister. Better yet, let me talk to her. I have a few things that I need to tell her about right now."

"No."

She waited for him to say that he was joking or to at least put her sister on the phone. But he didn't say anything at all for several seconds. When she told him again, the line went dead, and she couldn't believe what was going on with her family right now. Someone had actually hung up on her when she was trying her best to do right by them.

"I'm going to kill them all. Starting with that man." She realized that she hadn't gotten his name and was pissed about that too. Holding her head, she needed to lie down or be sick again before she dealt with anyone else in her family. They were all getting on her last nerve.

Her room was a mess. She'd had a temper tantrum earlier when one of her new dresses didn't fit her. They'd either given her the wrong size or something. Now, every article of clothing was lying on her floor, and a couple of drawers had been pulled out and emptied and scattered all over the room. Christ, she hated messes but was too sick to be able to find someone to take care of it now.

As soon as she laid down, she had to rush to the bathroom. It wasn't her lack of meds that was making her feel this way, but the anger she had toward her family. Throwing up several times, most of it bile, she crawled through her room's mess and laid on the rug that was by her bed. She couldn't get up another time.

As she laid there, plotting and planning, she thought of her sister again. Cass wasn't going to be able to get away with this today. She'd told her yesterday that she was going to start behaving or she'd have to take her to task. Cynthia had gotten a whip from the barn that she was going to use on Cass again if she didn't start doing what she'd been told.

When she woke up, she was slightly disorientated. Figuring out that she'd been on the floor to sleep didn't help her mood, but her head was feeling better. Going into the hallway, she found the maid coming out of her mother's office and told her she'd have to fix her room next. When she told her she'd get right on it, for some reason, she wanted to slap the shit right out of her. There was a tone there, and it bothered her that everyone was against her all the time. She was going to have to have a talk with Daddy about that as well. People were all against her, and she couldn't figure out why.

After getting herself something to eat, she was ready to face her sister and father. Daddy would have to side with her as he wasn't going to be around all that much longer, and she'd have to take over his duties as well. He'd better was all she could think about.

She was also going to have a word about his having this tumor, too. He was dragging her down all the time with his sad face and talking about how he was going to be dying soon. She wished he'd just get it over with and die already so that she could have the attention back on her again. His lingering around was just stupid. Perhaps she'd talk him into having the doctor speed things up for her, and that would be the end of him being so needy.

He'd not been. That was another thing she was going to have a talk to him about. He and Cass were always hanging out together. Playing that horse game. He'd never invited her to play the horse game, and she wasn't going to allow them to play anymore if they weren't going to invite her to play. There were plenty of pieces. They just have to make room for her. Writing that in her little notebook, she was going to have to have a talk with her daddy that lasted all night the way things were going right now.

~*~

Conri couldn't believe his luck tonight. He'd taken

Cass to the burger joint, and her dad was there getting him something to eat. He had explained that it was cook's night off, and he treated himself to a burger out when that happened. Also, he'd have a shake, he told them, but no fries. He didn't care all that much for them. Conri had been kidding when he told Cindy that he was enjoying them with his dinner.

"She has this notebook that she's writing things down in. Things that she wants to talk to you about, Dad." Before her dad had joined them, he had just asked Cass what was wrong with her. It took him ten minutes to find out that she'd been hit with a riding crop by her sister. And if that wasn't bad enough, she told him that she'd hit her with one before, but never had she drawn blood before. He was about as pissed off as he'd been about meeting her.

Cass was nothing like he'd imagined her to be. She was beautiful in every sense of the word. Her smile made his heart beat a little faster. The fact that she didn't need makeup or wear it led him to think that she was a natural beauty rather than a made-up one. Her voice, even when she was upset like she had been, wasn't shrill or loud. She calmly told him that she was upset with her sister and then that she'd been hit by her. Conri wanted to slay her dragons, but she asked him to wait. Not that she didn't want him to do anything about her sister, just to wait until she was in a better frame of mind to talk to him about her.

"I've seen her writing things in that little book of hers. She used to do it a lot when she was younger, keeping track of things that she wanted me to know about. It's only until recently that she's been writing things in it that have to do with things that she wants me to—I spoke to your brother on the way in here, and he said she's not taking her medications anymore. I'll have to speak to her about that, too. It's dangerous when she's not taking them. As you've witnessed first-hand." Conri asked what was wrong with her. "She's bipolar, for one, and she has a serious chemical imbalance too that when she's not taking her medication, she goes into this fight mode. Everything is against her, and she's the only one that can fix that. I should have noticed that myself and might have been able to nip this in the bud before now. If she refuses to take the medications, then she'll end up in an asylum again. This time for a lot longer than before. When she gets in that sort of mood, she's a danger to all of us and herself as well."

Conri didn't want to be afraid for Cass and her father, but he found himself being just that. If Cindy, as he'd been calling her, which Cass said that she hated, did anything else to his mate, she was going to have to deal with him. And that wasn't going to be pretty.

After dinner, he took Cass to his home. Mom

wanted to meet her, and while Cass wasn't keen on meeting his mom right now, she was polite and nice to her and his brothers. They seemed to be falling all over themselves, proving to her that they were there if she needed them.

That just pissed her off, and it was funny to see her tangle with the five of them when she'd had enough of them handling her. They were, too. Like a kitten or pup that they'd just gotten, and everyone wanted to hold her.

"Behave yourselves, or I'll teach you some manners." They each backed away after welcoming her to the family. "We'll see about that. I have my own family crisis to deal with right now. With my sister off her meds and my dad sick, I'm barely hanging on here. So just behave yourselves, and I might get to like you all."

Mom invited her to stay the night as they had plenty of room. She agreed that she didn't want to face her sister and her list right now but would have to call her parents and tell them where she was going to be. As she left the room to make her call, he looked at his brothers. He needed them to understand something as well.

"Howard said she was dangerous. Not only has she hit Cass with a riding crop, but she said she was going to ruin my face as well. I'm taking this very seriously right now. Especially if her sister is saying that she was going to kill Cass if she dated me." Yuri told them again about her insisting that she date him before Cass, and it really bothered him that she wouldn't take no for an answer. "If you see her out and about, though Howard said that she's not much of a townie person, but if you see her in town, avoid her at all costs. And I'd like for you guys to keep an eye on Cass and Mom while they're out without me."

"You think that she really will hurt Cass?" He explained that she already had. "I know that, but I mean, do you think she'll kill her given the chance? If that's right, then you have to proclaim her as your mate soon. It'll give her immortality and save you the heartache of losing her."

That's how they'd been able to get their father and Carol out of their lives. Conri hadn't ever proclaimed her as his. They'd slept together and had had a lot of sex in those first few months, but he'd never claimed her as his own. So, she was never given immortality. Mom had claimed that she no longer wanted to be regarded as a mate to his father. That took away his immortality, too, when it was needed to seek pack judgment against him. It had been a bit more complicated about their father, but once it was finished, he was as well.

"I don't want to rush her." He had a feeling that

she'd not be rushed into anything. After she came back into the room, he was happy when she sat down next to him. "Is everything all right with your family?"

"Yes. Dad convinced Mom to meet him in town, and they're going to stay at the bed and breakfast for a few days. They've not told Cynthia and don't plan on it. But my brother knows, so he won't tell her. Mom said that she threatened to kill me and Conri if I was really dating him. Is that what we call this between us? Dating?"

"We can call it that for now. But as my mate, in our pack or any other pack, we're considered to be married. Nothing will come between us so long as — we'll live forever if you were to tell me that it's all right to claim you." She didn't immediately tell him no, for which he was grateful. But she did ask him what that meant. "I just say to a group of wolves that I claim you as my mate for all time. It'll make you safer being around your sister. Also, you won't gain any weight — unless you're breeding, nor will you get sick with any human diseases, either. Plus, while I don't know how much or what it would be, you'll get a bit of magic too — more so because you'll be the female version of myself as alpha."

"Can I think on that? At least for the night?" He told her that it would be totally up to her. But she shouldn't just not take it because they don't know one another just yet. "I understand that you're trying to protect me from Cynthia, and I will admit that I'm afraid that she'll hurt me. I just need to think about what that will mean to the rest of my family and their not being immortal. They can't be, can they?"

"No, I'm sorry. I can't give it to them unless the king of our kind says it's all right. I can contact him and ask him about it. I know about your father. But that will be completely up to him." She said that is why she wanted to think about it. "All right, you think about it, and I'll do my very best not to piss you off any more than I already have."

The rest of the evening was spent getting to know each other. His brothers, one by one, headed to their own homes, and since he was living in the pack house with his mom, he only had to show her the rooms of the place and let her pick out one for herself. He was glad when she took the old room that he had. Having her sleeping in his old bed was something akin to having her in his big bed in the master suite of the house. Conri felt like if anyone heard what he'd been thinking, they'd never let him live it down.

Going to bed that night, he had to sit down when he thought of her being his mate. He'd gone to see her pissed off, and the little bit of time that he'd spent with her had him changing his mind about everything. While eating with her, he'd probed her mind for anything that he'd found in Carol's mind, and all he could find was that she wasn't lying to him and she didn't know what it meant to be his mate. Just honesty was all he found, too.

Getting up when all he was doing was tossing and turning, he pulled out his laptop and began a search on her family. And because he ran background checks on everyone who worked in the house, he did one on her and her sister. Howie, too, but he could only find that he'd been married once before and that six months after they were wed, there had been a horrific accident that had taken her life and that of their unborn child.

Cynthia was a different story. There were so many articles in the newspaper that he was surprised to know that she'd been released from the hospital for the criminally insane. She'd killed four people one afternoon when she couldn't get in touch with her father. She believed that the four people who had died by her hand were keeping him from her. He read the article about her trial.

She'd been deemed unfit to stand trial. Her thinking was that it had been all right for her to have killed those people because she'd not been able to find her father. The article went on to say that they'd had to lock her up and put her into restraints before they finally got her on the medication that she needed. Cynthia had only been out on her own for the last ten years. She was deemed fit so long as she took her meds on time and was monitored daily by a doctor. He'd bet anything that no one had been to see her in a few months and not have anyone notice that she'd been acting up again.

He made a mental note to ask Cass about it when he saw her in the morning. He also wondered if that was the reason she didn't live at home, that Cass was somehow a trigger for the older woman. Another thing that he was going to talk to her about. Just as he was closing up his computer, there was a knock at the door. Going to get it, he was glad that he'd not undressed completely when he'd gotten in the room. It was his mom.

"I remembered that I had this cleaned for you a couple of months ago." She handed him the small box from the jeweler. "I thought that if she allows you to claim her, you should give her a ring, too. It's one that your father didn't give me, but I purchased it for myself."

The ring was a simple band that had a wolf's paw print on the inside of the ring. There was a slit in it for someone to be able to shift and not lose a finger while doing it. He didn't know why, but he had a feeling that Cass would like this ring over any diamond that he could give her. She'd not like cut flowers either, he thought. She would prefer plants over cut ones.

"I love it, Mom. Thank you very much." She nodded once and then began to walk away. "Do you like her?" She asked if that was important to him. "Yes. She's my mate, but I want her to be liked by the family. Especially by you."

"I do like her. She's very friendly but knows when to cut you guys off when she gets upset. She's not an angry person either. Just calm and, like you said, not loud when she's upset. I hope she allows you to claim her, son. I don't want anything to happen to her either." He said he wasn't going to force her into anything. "Good for you. I do like her and hope that I can come to love her as much as you will be in love with her. There haven't been any women around here for far too long now. It'll be a nice change for her to be a part of the family. But I am worried about her sister."

"I was looking her up. She's been put away for murder. I didn't see how long she was away, but I have a feeling that it was a few years. I also think that somehow Cass isn't joking when she said she's afraid of her. She's scary." Mom said she thought so as well. "Be careful when you're out and about. She more than likely doesn't know who you are yet, but just be careful. I couldn't stand for anything to happen to you or any of the others."

"I will." She hugged him then, and it felt good. "I'm going to be in town in the morning for a couple of meetings. The two of you will need to get Cass settled someplace where she's safe like her parents have."

"Thanks again for the ring, Mom. I know she'll love it." At least, he hoped that she would. He didn't know much about women and less about his mate, but he had a feeling that she was going to like the simpler things in life rather than her sister, liking to be the center of attention all the time.

Chapter 4

Howard answered his phone and immediately regretted it. It was Cynthia again. She'd left so many messages on his cell phone that he couldn't get through them all without sitting down for an hour. And with each one of them, she got angrier and angrier.

She started out being angry with just Cass. Then, as the messages progressed, she was mad at him and Howie too. He never figured out what she was mad at her brother about, something about him being twenty-nine, but she was very clear on what Cass had done to her to piss her off.

"Where are you, Daddy?" He'd never hated a name as much as he did her calling him 'Daddy.' Maybe if she was five or so, but not a forty-year-old woman calling him that. "I've been looking for you and Mother for days on end, and I can't find you. You're on my list now, Daddy. You don't want to be on my list."

"No, I'm sure that I don't. Where are you, Cynthia? Have you decided to get back on your meds? You'd better, or you're going to be sick again. You remember the last time, don't you? How sick you got when you'd get those headaches?" She told him that she was never going back on them again. They made her feel doped up all the time. "That's why you take them. They keep you calm. You need to be calm, and all the headaches will go away."

"I don't want to talk to you about medication, Daddy. I want to know what it is you're going to be doing about Mother and Cass. They're into things together, and I need for you to put a stop to it." He asked what they were doing together. "Plotting my demise. Not really. I'm stronger than they are. Smarter too. I want you to divorce mother. That's the only way to keep her out of my business. And Cass needs to be put down."

"Put down? I don't think I want to understand what you mean by that, Cynthia. And I will not divorce your mother. You do know that she'll still be your mother if I were to divorce her, don't you?" She told him that she was messing in her business. "I don't think she's messing in anything that you're doing. I want to talk to you about your medications. You need to start taking them again."

"Stop bringing up the fucking medications." Her voice echoed in his mind. Her anger was almost palpable to him. "Now, what are you going to do about Cass? She's dating, and I've not given her permission to do so. I've told her and told her that she's not to date men until I don't want them. Then she can date my sloppy seconds. After I've had them, they won't want to downgrade to someone like her. Howie won't get involved unless she starts dating the people he's dating. That's the point I'm trying to make with her. No one wants her after they've been with me, and that's the way it has to work."

She was making no sense. What did Howie have to do? Dating women? Nothing that she said was clear to him, and he was going to have to nail her down a bit to get clearer answers. Before he could, however, she was on again about rules that Cass wasn't following, and somehow that was her mother's fault.

"Calm down, Cynthia. You're confusing me. What are you going on about with rules?" She was calm for the briefest of moments. "Now tell me what's this about rules. I don't understand which rules she's breaking."

"All of them. I have rules, and she's not following any of them, Daddy. She's supposed to be living here, and I haven't seen her in days to explain to her about coming in late. She's to not date unless I say it's all right." She growled low in her throat, and it made him think of a caged animal. A wild one at that. "I just know she's seeing those Valley men and fucking them. There isn't to be any of that either. Not until I'm finished with them. I want her to hand over her phone to me so that I can monitor her calls. She's keeping me in the dark about her life. I won't have it."

"She's a grown woman, the same as you are. I don't even want to know what she has on her phone. Or if she's...why do you care who she's seeing? It's frankly none of your business who she's with. And the young man that she's seeing is a nice man." He knew his mistake as soon as the words left his mouth. "His name is Conri, and he's going to marry her. Now, that's going to happen and —"

"She. Is. Not to. Date. Anyone. Until. I say. So. Did you understand me that time? Do I fucking have to spell it for you next? Not anyone, and she will not marry before me. Christ, you're off your rocker, Daddy. You're lingering around is going to cause me trouble. I'm going to have to talk to your doctor about speeding up your death. I hate that too, but you're messing things up now, and I will have to take charge." He didn't hear anything past her telling him she wished that he'd hurry up and die.

Closing his cell phone, he laid it as gently as he could on the table that was in the room they were renting. She wanted him to hurry up and die. And he had no doubt that she'd call his doctor if she ever found out who he was. And she'd tell him just what she said she would. She wanted him dead. When the phone rang again, he calmly picked it up and broke it in half. He wasn't going to speak to her again, not without witnesses. He almost didn't believe his own ears when he thought about what she'd said to him.

When Elizabeth came back from shopping, careful to never be alone in their own town, he told her everything that had been said and how she wanted Cass to be put down. She was just as shocked as he'd been.

"I don't know what to do now. She needs to be put back in that asylum. Never to be let out—I don't know why they ever thought it was a good idea to let her out in the first place. They were able to keep her on her meds. And that fool of a doctor said he could monitor from her cell phone. Obviously, that didn't work. She's back to being like she was only worse. At least then we could calm her down by just talking to her." Elizabeth agreed with him, but he could see the worry on her face. "We'll have to make some calls. Get her back where she was before she hurts someone or kills them."

It took them nearly an hour to get back with the doctor that had taken care of her in the asylum. He was just as shocked as they'd been when the other doctor, the one who was supposed to keep an eye on her, was doing it from her cell phone.

"Where is she now?" They told him that she was at their home. "We'll get with the police to be able to take her in quietly. I don't want her to be harmed, nor do I want anyone else to be harmed. We'll have to sedate her to bring her in."

Arrangements were made to get the police involved and how they were going to do it. Howard felt terrible that it had had to be done this way and held onto his wife for support. They didn't have a choice in the matter. Cynthia was a danger to herself and others. Next, he had to call Cass and Howie to let them know what was going on. Cass answered first, and then they brought their son in on the call, as well as Conri.

After telling them everything that was going on, including the phone call with Cynthia, they asked questions about how it was going to work. Conri said that he could have some of his pack there that would help the police if he wanted, and he was all for that. The more help they had, the better things would go, he thought.

"I've spoken to the police here in town. The doctor told them that it would be better to try talking to her in the morning. Before she has time to go over her notes. We're going to meet them at the house at dawn to make sure that she's at home." Howard told Conri that she never leaves the house. "We just want to make sure that she stays there if she's there or find her if she's not. As you said, there is no way of knowing what she's been up to while living there alone for the past week. I'm to understand that the staff has left, too."

"The men are still taking care of the horses, but they're far from the house. I don't know that she'd go down there at all. She feels that the place is beneath her and dirty. The one and only time I know she's been there was when she was looking for me." Howard thought again about how she called him 'daddy' all the time and had to swallow a bit of his grief for what could happen out at the house tomorrow. "You'll keep us informed, won't you, Conri? And Cass, you and Howie should come here to stay with us. I'd feel better if you were both here where I can watch over you."

"I can be there, Dad." After Howie spoke, Cass said that she'd be there as well. "Dad, you just make sure you are going to be all right, too. I don't want anything to happen to you two either."

"Thank you, son. I'm going to rest tonight. This has been so stressful for us all. I'm going to have to get me a new number and phone soon. I can't stand to listen to her anymore. I broke my phone after the last time she called me." Howard held onto his wife's hands and told the kids how much he loved them. "Conri, you make sure that you're not hurt either. You've only just become a part of the family, and I can't stand for anything to happen to you, too."

That night, when they were getting ready for

bed, he cried softly into his pillow. He hurt for his children and, especially, Cass. She'd done nothing wrong to bring this down on her head, and Cynthia was blaming all her woes on her. He thought about how Cass had been asked to move out, and it hurt his heart every time he thought about it.

She'd lived in the big house for all her life. When she'd turned fourteen, she and Cynthia never had a cross word until then. He thought that she'd found competition in her little sister, but Cass was too busy forming her own way in the world to be bothered by her sister's complaints. Then, one night, Cynthia had gotten violent with Cass.

Cass spent the next month in the hospital recovering from the wounds that her older sister had inflicted on her. She had drugged her with one of her own tablets and then tied her up. Finding her tied to her bed and Cynthia standing over her with a bloodied riding crop had nearly done him in.

She'd hit her with it fifty-seven times before she'd been caught, and only then because Cass had woken up and was screaming. He didn't want to think about the things that had spewed from her mouth when the police had come to take her away. He had no doubt that this time would be no different, with her saying things that were never true about Cass.

"Are you asleep?" He told his lovely wife that

he wasn't and didn't know if he could. "Yes, me either. I keep thinking about the things she'd said to me that morning that I left. She was set to kill me. Or have you do it. She told me that you loved her more than you did me." He said that wasn't true. "Yes, I know that love, but she was saying things that I believe will haunt me for the rest of my life. She hated me that much, enough to have said you were going to take care of me." He felt her shiver.

"I never gave into her like she says I did. Like I was the only one to be able to make things right for her. I just don't know where she got that." Elizabeth said she'd never been a daddy's girl. "No, not at all. And I hate that she calls me 'Daddy' all the time. I've tried to tell her she was too old to be calling me that, but she wouldn't have it. Like she was just a child, calling me that."

"She's called me Elizabeth for the last few years. I didn't mind that so much as her calling me 'Mommy.' You're right. I hated her calling you 'Daddy' too. I thought that it was very immature of her. Do you believe that she's going to be forty-one soon? And we've always been slightly afraid of her. At least I have been. Sometimes, she looks at me like she's wondering where to stick the knife." She shivered again. "I can't get over how much she's taken over our lives. We're supposed to be in our golden years right now, not having the police go in and arrest her because we're afraid of her. And I am, too. How about you, honey?"

"I've been afraid of her since she hurt Cass. If she could do that to her own sister, there is no telling what she could do to us." He pulled his wife into his arms and held her. "We'll make sure that she doesn't get out this time. I don't care if we have to pay with every penny we have. She won't get out to hurt any of us again."

"No, you're right. We can't live like this. And with you only...I'm going to miss you so much, Howard. I just don't know what I'm going to do with myself." He held her while she cried softly. His own heart was breaking, too. If only, he thought they'd of found it sooner, he might be around a bit more. Just a little more time to see Conri and his Cass's children.

~*~

Conri was nervous about this whole thing. Not only was Cindy not at home, but she wasn't at the horse barns either. He had his brothers go around as their wolves to find her, but so far, no one was having any luck. Conri was the most worried about Cass and the fact that he'd never claimed her as yet. Too much going on. And now he had every reason to wish he'd just done it to keep her safe.

The two of them were getting along better than he'd ever had with Carol. She'd been spending a lot of time with her father, for which he couldn't blame her. She had the kind of dad that he thought he would have loved to have. Even Elizabeth was someone that he loved to be around. It had only taken him a couple of times being at the bed and breakfast together that he'd fallen in love with the entire family.

He knew that he loved Cass, too. She was funny and articulate. She could play chess and wasn't a sore loser when he did manage to beat her. Just hanging around them all made his days seem to go better. His mood had improved as well.

Cass wore the ring that his mom had given him. And just as he'd thought, she loved the plainness of it. When asked if she wanted something different or even bigger, she told him no, the one that he'd given her was perfect. A couple of days ago, he'd even stopped comparing her to Carol as much as he had been. She was just Cass Warmer Valley, and he'd fallen head over heels in love with her.

"I'm not finding her scent anywhere around the house. I mean, not even at the doors. I'm thinking that she has to be inside and we've just missed her. Her scent is the strongest in the house, too." He said that they searched every room in the place. *"I don't know. Perhaps call Howard and find out if they have a secret room or maybe a cellar that we didn't find."*

"Give me five minutes, and I'll call him. Just be careful

of her. She could just sneak up on you in a heartbeat." Conri called Elizabeth as Howard still didn't have a phone. When she answered, he had a feeling that something was wrong. "Is she there with you, Elizabeth?" Her whispered answer made his wolf snarl at him.

"She's just outside the building. It's like she knows we're in here but is teasing us until she comes inside." He asked where the others were. "We're all huddled up in the bathroom. Don't ask me why, but that seemed to be the most logical place. However, now that I think about it, it's also a good place for her to get to us all at once."

"You're right. Go into the little lounge. Just be careful. I'm sending my brothers and the police to you. Don't be alarmed if you see some wolves. My brothers will be safer as their other half." She said for him to hurry. "I'm speaking to them now." After telling them where Cindy was, they took off towards town. Then he spoke to the police.

Since they knew that they were wolves, too, they knew not to be freaked out by seeing them either. Catching a ride with the police, leaving two behind in the event she got away from them, he couldn't get the officer to go fast enough for him. He was right. They didn't need to get into a crash before getting there. But he was worried about Cass.

"When we get home today, if we do, then I want you

to claim me in whatever way will make me the safest. I can't protect my family, being just a puny human. I should have thought of that sooner." He was so glad to hear from Cass that he nearly shifted to be with her sooner. He told her what was going on with the police. *"You stay out of harm's way, too. I know my sister well enough to know that she'll hurt you if given the chance."*

"I am. I promise that I don't want to be hurt either. But if she harms you in any way, I'm going for her ass." She told him she was glad to hear that, which surprised him to no end. She was her sister, after all. *"I just heard from Rette. He said they're coming up on the bed and breakfast now. Stay alert."* She said that she would but to stop talking to her so she could pay attention to what was going on around her.

The police were there when they pulled into the street across from the place. They had spread out all over the big home and were waiting for orders. He'd gotten to the point that he just wanted her out of their lives, but it wasn't his decision to make. When Lamar said she was coming around the front, he watched her as she came around the building with her empty hands up and a huge smile on her face. There was something so not right about that.

Cindy was arrested without incident. She still hadn't spoken to anyone by the time she was put into the car but to ask for her daddy. He went into the place to make sure that the Warmer family was all right. Things couldn't have been better when Cass leapt into his arms and hugged him.

"Everyone all right?" They said they were, but he still checked them all out. "She's asking to see you, Howard. The police are saying that it's up to you. They have her in shackles and arm restraints. The doctors are waiting for the ambulance to come to take her with them."

"I don't want to see her." He nodded. "Do you think I'm a terrible person for not seeing my daughter, Conri?"

"What I think doesn't matter. However, I would say that if you don't see her, I wouldn't blame you one bit. She's caused enough trouble over three lifetimes to warrant what you're saying. Also, I'm going to say this now. I don't believe for a minute that she's going to be this easy to take care of. She's planning something. I can feel it in my bones." Just as he was helping them leave the room, he felt the ground rumble under his feet. Then, a second time.

"Christ, what was that?" They all scrambled to get out of the house and into the streets. Whatever it had been, there was another explosion and another rolling of people around. Just as he was thinking that it sounded like a bomb went off, Yuri, who had stayed at the Warmer home in the event that Cindy returned, contacted him.

"*It's gone. Conri, the entire house is gone.*" He asked him what he was talking about. "*The house and one of the smaller barns up close to the house have exploded. We felt it all the way out to the horse barns. It's just in splinters still tumbling down onto the remains.*" He pulled Cass into his arms and told her in whispers what Yuri was telling him.

"No, she didn't do it. Please tell me that she didn't just blow up our home." They both looked in the cruiser that she was sitting in the back of. Cindy was laughing hard and pounding her fist against the window. He didn't know how she'd done it, but he knew that she'd just destroyed the home of her parents.

Telling the Warmers that their house was gone nearly took them all three to the floor. There had been police in the house not thirty minutes ago. His brother could have been closer to the house and been hurt badly. He wanted to pull Cindy from the car and make her tell him why she'd done such a thing. People could have been killed.

When she was taken away in the ambulance and heavily sedated, they all didn't say anything. Almost as soon as Howard came up to him, he nearly missed grabbing him up before he fell down. The man was a mess, and so was his family. Cass was telling them that they could stay with them until they rebuilt. If they rebuilt. He couldn't imagine the things, small and large treasures they would have lost in this senseless act of violence.

"*I'm telling my parents they can stay with us in your home. I should have asked, but I didn't think about it not being mine.*" He said that everything that he had was now hers. "*Thank you for that. But I still should have asked.*"

"*Tell them there is plenty of room, and we'll get the insurance company on it right away. Yuri said the horses were all right, if not slightly startled. I'm just so glad that no one was home. I wonder if she had figured that into...I can't believe that she did this to their home.*" She told him she couldn't believe it either. "*I have to keep telling myself that no one was hurt. Yuri told me that everything is gone.*

Everyone followed the fire trucks out to the ranch. There really wasn't anything to see. Like Yuri said, the house was totally destroyed. The little fires that were still burning were easy enough to get under control. Howie knew enough to call the vet and have him come out and check on the horses.

"We have nothing but the few clothes that we took to the bed and breakfast with us. Nothing else. No photo albums. None of the blankets that were made by my mom's and Howard's. It's all gone. Oh, my jewelry, too." Elizabeth looked up at him. "Things keep popping into my head that we lost, but I have to keep telling myself that we're all right, all of us are."

"And you'll be staying with us in the house until you get things figured out." She said she didn't want to put him out. "You won't. The pack house is big because it has room for families that have had something happen to their home, and they stay there. My mom doesn't live there anymore. It's just me and Cass, and she is staying in another bedroom from mine." She thanked him for that.

"As soon as your insurance company says it's all right, we'll get a construction crew out here to clean this up and get started on the rebuild. I'm assuming that you'd like to start fresh, new home and all." She told him they'd been thinking of remodeling the house for a few years now. "Well, now you can. "It'll be cheaper to start this way from what I told. No places that you have to work around."

"Are you always this upbeat and positive?" Conri told her that only since he'd met Cass. Before that, he couldn't stand to be around humans at all. "Yes, well, I just have to remember that staying positive can go a long way. Right now, all I want is a bed and a shower. For as much fun as it was staying with the kids last night, they wore me out. As I said, too much positive is just too much." She looked at him again and cried. "You're a good man, Conri. The best person I can think of for my little girl, too. Thank you."

"You're so very welcome." He grabbed Cass as she was going by him and smiled. "Cassidy Lynne Warmer Valley, I pronounce on this day that you are my mate and give you all that I have from this day forward. Standing here in front of witness, I proclaim you as my mate."

She swayed on her feet for a few seconds before she grabbed him by his arms. He could see her face and knew that she was getting magic from him. When she grinned at him, he wondered what she'd do now.

"Conri James Valley, I pronounce on this day that you are my mate and give you all that I have from this day forward. Standing here in front of witness, I proclaim you as my mate." She looked up at him and then laid her head on his chest. "Did I do it right? Your mom helped me with your middle name, and I've been practicing all this week for when we had time. I figured that if you didn't do it soon, I'd just take you as my mate and see how that worked for you."

"Are you going to be like this all the time, staying one or two steps ahead of me?" She told him that she was going to try. "Good. I like that in a mate. I'm in love with you, Cass."

"And I'm in love with you." She was congratulated and hugged by everyone around them, including the police, who had come out to the house with them. "Now, let's get my family home so that they can rest up. I have a feeling that the next few days are going to be hectic trying to figure out what else Cynthia has done."

"Do you think that she's done more than this?" Cass told her dad that she had no reason to believe that she'd done a few things in the name of destroying things that belonged to the family. "Oh my, I never… well, I never thought she'd blow up our family home, but here she's done it. Yes, you might be right in thinking that we have plenty more to look for. It's a scary thought, too, to think that she's been plotting things out in that head of hers. At least we don't have to worry about her getting to us anymore."

"I wouldn't even rule that out, Dad. There was something just too easy about her giving up. I don't believe for a moment she thinks that she's done. No way would she have gone away quietly. I think for the next few weeks, we keep on our toes and look out for her still." Howard said that he would. "I don't mean just her physically showing up, Dad, but something that she might well have done, and it needs to…well needs to go off yet. Remember, she's still plotting and planning. And I have been the source of her plans for long enough to know that she's coming for me one way or the other."

Conri hoped that she was wrong, but he also believed that she would still be coming around. Her planning had already taken out an entire house and barn.

Chapter 5

Cynthia thought her plan was going well. Since they weren't at the other house, they had to be in the one that she'd been in, the big house. But they'd been at the little house — no, no. She couldn't confuse herself now. They were all dead, and it was just her. The only person she wasn't sure of was Cass. She'd been there when she was arrested. Things were getting all muddled up in her head, and she was having difficulty keeping things straight.

She was currently strapped to a cot. Not a bed like she wanted but a cot that was too narrow by half and harder than her head. When she saw the doctor coming toward her, she made herself look pitiful. She knew that she could fool him, the little bastard.

"Ms. Warmer, I see that you're back. Good for you. I never thought that you should have been sent from here in the first place. We'll get you up and going in a few weeks as soon as we get your medications in you for a week or two." She had to act like she was taking the meds so that she could be ready when Cass came to visit her. And she would. Just like she had before. "We're going to have to keep a better eye on you this time. No more not taking your meds. We have a solution for that now. We have them in injections."

'What? No,' she screamed in her mind. Shots would be more difficult to not take. She needed to make sure they came in pill form. Opening her mouth when she was told it was time to get her started on them, the doctor just laughed.

The pinch to her arm nearly had her acting out again. She had to maintain a clear-headed sister so that when Cass came to see her, she'd be able to kill her. And then there would be no more troubles with her sister. She'd be free to do what she wanted. And dating was going to be the first thing on her list of things to do that Cass could no longer do. Cynthia knew her plan would work. Just like it did at the house.

But it had blown up too soon. She'd meant for them all to be in the house when it went up. Now, she didn't know. Didn't know. Didn't know. Cynthia felt the medication starting to make her not be able to think again. She'd be doped up for days on end if they kept injecting her with drugs without her permission.

Her Daddy was the last thing she thought of when the drugs took her under. Mother fuckers. She was going to have to do something to get her back on the pills.

When she woke up, she was in a room. There

was wallpaper on the walls that looked familiar, but she couldn't remember where it was from. Looking around with just her eyes, she nearly screamed when her daddy was in the room. He was supposed to be dead, damn it.

"You're not talking to me? I suppose that's fine. I have a few things to say to you, then I'm leaving here never to return." She tried to reach out to her daddy, but she was strapped down with both her legs and arms. Jerking on them, she looked at her daddy. "Why did you blow up the house? There was no reason for it. No one was there, so I don't know your plans."

"You were all supposed to be there." Against her will, she told him why she'd taken care of the house. "Why weren't you there, Daddy? You never do what I want. It's always about Cass, isn't it? You love her more than me."

"You wanted me dead?" She told him that she wanted them all dead. "Why? Why would you want such a thing? We're your family, Cynthia."

"If you're all dead, the attention would forever be on me. They'd have to like me more because Cass was dead and gone. Don't you see? It's got to be all about me all the time. You'd want me to have that, wouldn't you, Daddy? Have the attention all on me?" He didn't say anything. "Good. Now, here is what I want you to do. I want you to kill Cass and that boyfriend of hers. Kill them both dead. Howie will have to go, too. He's been having too much attention on him since I killed Margaret and their baby. I thought that people would…well, it matters little now, but you'll have to kill him off, too. Then you kill Mommy. She's worthless anyway, never wanting to show me off. After you kill Mommy, then you'll kill yourself. Or have the police do it. Oh yes, that's it. Have the police kill you because you killed all the other people."

"You killed Margaret and her unborn child? I don't want to believe that, Cynthia. Why would you do something like that?" She said that Margaret was hogging all the attention with her fat belly. He wasn't paying attention to her, and she told him that. "That's all you've ever wanted was attention, isn't it? You never wanted anyone to outshine you."

"You're finally getting it. No one should be above me in attention getting. I've worked really hard on that, and when people get in my way like Margaret did, I just take care of it. But since you didn't die when I wanted you to, you're going to do what I say and make sure that everyone will feel sorry for me for having such a fucked up father. I might even have to tell them that you abused me when things wind down a bit after you're dead." She didn't understand the look on his face, so she thought that he was still finally understanding what she wanted. "When do you think you can get started on Cass and her boyfriend? You'll have to plan things perfectly so you don't get caught before you take care of yourself and Mommy. Oh, and Howie. Don't forget to take care that he's dead as well. I've never forgiven him for telling me that Margaret's death wasn't all about me. Well, you've no idea how much I wanted to tell him that I'd done it. But I didn't. Daddy — where are you going? You've never answered me about when you were going to start on Cass being dead."

"I don't know you anymore. You've killed our daughter-in-law and our grandson." Daddy backed away from her more. She didn't understand why he was upset. "You're not right in the head, Cynthia. There is something so...so...I don't know what to call it, but that you're a murderer."

"Well, duh. I've done it before. And think about it, Daddy, we'll be the same, you and I. I can't believe that you and I will be the same thing. Murderers. I already know how you're going to go down. They'll blame it on your tumor. They'll tell me how sorry they are that you did this to my entire family. Don't you see? It's going to be the best gift you've ever given me. I love you, Daddy." He jerked back when she reached for him. She didn't know what was wrong with him all of the sudden, but she was going to make sure that he understood this was for him, too. "You won't have to be killed by me if you do this right, Daddy. Like I said, they'll blame it on your tumor, and that will be what people talk about to me. How the thing in your head made you a monster. But we don't want too much of the attention on you. That will just make me mad, and no one wants me to be mad at them. Just do what I tell you, and you'll make me—"

"I'm not killing anyone. I don't know where you—I don't understand you at all. I mean, I knew that you liked to be the center of attention. That's why I had Cassidy move out, so that—you're not right in the head." He seemed to come to some kind of resolution then, and she knew he had thought it through and was going to give it all to her. "No, I'm not going to kill my children or my wife. I don't know where you got the thought that I'd do something like that. No. Just no."

He left her there. No matter how much she yelled for him to come back, he wouldn't do it. She told herself that he needed to think about it for a little while before he committed himself to giving her the best gift of all. She forgot to ask him about insurance money. She was going to need some cash before too much longer. Yes, he'd do it because he liked giving her things that she wanted. And this would be the best of all presents.

She must have dozed off or something because when she woke, she was alone in the room.

Remembering her Daddy and what he was going to do for her made her giddy with excitement. There might even be something on the news about it. When the nurse came into her room, she asked for a newspaper or a television. How else would she know that he'd started already but by seeing it or reading about it? After another shot in her arm, she really was going to have to do something about that. She started to doze off again.

Daddy was going to do it. He was going to make this happen for her. She just knew it. Then she'd be so happy. Making sure she looked her best, she didn't want the police, when they came to tell her about the murders, to be appalled at her appearance. She let the drugs take her under.

Waking up again, making sure that she was alone in the room again, she smiled when she thought of her Daddy making things happen for her. He should just want to do things for her as she'd been his beautiful daughter. She didn't count Cass, hoping by now that she was dead.

Trying to move around on the cot, she realized she was still chained up. It was frustrating for her that she had to continue on this ruse to make people here think that she was insane. She wasn't and realized that she should have had her Daddy make sure to tell them that she was as sane as anybody else. She would get out when the time was right, she supposed. But the waiting was going to be hard on her. Cynthia liked to have her plans all laid out in a neat row before she could start on them, like the thing with her Daddy. He'd do it even if it was only for her. She was and had always been a daddy's little girl, and now was no different. Her door opened, and she saw it was one of the male attendants.

"It's time to eat your supper, Ms. Warmer." She held up her hands for him to remove the cuffs. Her legs would have to be loosened, too, because she had to pee. "No, I'm going to feed you today. You have to go to the bathroom? If so, I need to get a bedpan for you."

"I'm not pissing in the bed. Let me up so that I can do it by myself." He told her she wasn't going to be released, if ever. "What's that supposed to mean? I have to be released. I'm as sane as you are." He laughed.

"You're going to be locked down for the rest of your life after the stunt you tried to pull. By the way, I'm to tell you that none of your family will ever come to visit you. Your father told the head administrator what you told him to do. He said he's not going to do it, but he wanted to give us a heads up about you never leaving here. I think that's a safe bet now." She told him that was told in confidence. "You're being recorded twenty-four/seven now. Everyone is. I guess it sucks to be you."

When he started shoveling in her food, she didn't get to say anything else. She wanted to spit it in his face, but she'd learned not to do that the last time she was here. They held her food, and being on the restrictions like she was, he might not come to her when she needed to pee, like she did now.

It was humiliating to have someone lift you up so that you could get on a bedpan. He was making sure that she didn't get her gown wet, so he had it pulled up to her breasts. And since she was chained up, he had to wipe her, too. She'd never felt so embarrassed in her life as she was at this moment. When he finished, he actually praised her for having so much urine. Christ, she was going to kill this mother fucker as soon as she was released. There was no point in her being chained up like an animal. She was a grown assed woman.

When he finally left her, a nurse came into her room telling her it was time for her medications. This time, she was able to ask why they were keeping her drugged up when she was so obviously fine. She told her that she was to take her medications every six hours until she heard differently from the doctor.

"But I'd not count on him changing things up for you. Your father said you wanted him to kill your family so that you can be the center of attention." Cynthia said that was made in private. "There isn't anything you do or say that is private anymore. You're being recorded, voice too, all the time. But especially when you have visitors. But you're not likely to get any more of those now, are you? Your father said that none of them were coming here ever again. We've been told about your plot to have him kill off your brother and sister. Even your mom. He won't do it. Just so you know. He's a nice man and wouldn't do that kind of thing ever."

Surely, her daddy would do it. He agreed that he would. Well, maybe he didn't agree, but he didn't tell her that he'd not do it. But the more she thought about it, she came to the realization that he had told her that he'd never do it. Did that mean that he didn't love her anymore? She for sure knew that it meant that Cass would still be around. And getting all the attention that she could get for herself. Damn it all to fuck and back. Why were they all treating her this way?

~*~

Conri put the phone back on the cradle. He looked at Cass and decided that he wasn't going to keep anything from her. Starting right now with telling her about the things that happened with her dad today. The man was distraught and angry. And he didn't know that he'd be feeling the same way if it had happened to him.

"Before you tell me, I want you to know that I'm not as fragile as I looked. I mean, I might be small — though I think everyone is small compared to you — but I might be small, but I've been dealing with Cynthia all my life. So that being said, what did she do to my dad?" He told her everything. Including the part where he was to kill them both so that she'd be the center of attention. "Okay, that's a bit more than I think...did she really ask my dad to kill us?"

"Yes. And I forgot to mention that she's claiming that she killed Margaret and her unborn son, too. I think that has your dad the most upset. That she'd killed an innocent child." The tears were streaming down her face, and he so wanted her to not be upset about her sister anymore. "I'm sorry, love. I truly am. I can't believe that she was ever released in the first place."

"Something about her being a model patient. I think she was planning on getting out so that she could harm me. She's not liked me since I got boobs." The burst of laughter had her glaring at him. Then she laughed, too. "I'm sorry. I could have said that differently, but that's when it all started with her not liking me. She used to hurt me, too. Then, when Dad came to me about moving in with my Grandma, I leapt at the chance. So when I turned seventeen, and grandma died, I just stayed in her house with plans of staying there until I got out of college."

"What sort of things did she do to hurt you? I

mean, you were just a kid when she got out the first time, weren't you?" She told him that she was just shy of being sixteen. "Not a child at all. I'm sure it must have been hard on you."

"She cut my hair once. If I'd not been paying attention to things going on around me, I might well have been bald. I was taking driving lessons, and she cut the lines to the brakes. That was scary and would have been dangerous, but the driving instructor was driving at that time. She confessed to that by being pissed off because I wasn't killed. She tried to set fire to me once. The things she did to me never hurt me all that much because I'd learned to be on alert around her. I was never relaxed when she was pretending to be nice, either. She couldn't fool me." He told her he was sorry. "So am I. We could have been such great friends, I think. Maybe not. It's hard to tell with her. Mom would come and see me at Grandma's just to get away from her. She was constantly wanting her to take Cynthia out to lunch at the county club in Newark. She didn't even have a membership there. The funny part is, she just wanted mom to crash the place so that it would be all over the news at how this deranged mother wanted her daughter to be seen by country club people."

"And now she's been put away indefinitely. Your dad is to be notified if they think about releasing her. I would imagine that it would take a lot for her to be getting out now. What with the things that she did to the house and wanting to kill your family." Cass told him that she'd killed before, and they let her out. "I guess that's true. I never heard of her until now. I mean, wouldn't it have been in the newspaper?"

"That was Dad. He didn't want to hurt my brother's chances at becoming Mayor. Howie would have been good as Mayor of his town, but after Margaret was killed, he just never recovered. I don't know what it's going to do to him when he finds out that she killed his wife and child. Margaret was almost eight months pregnant at the time.

He held her in his arms when she began crying again. It was all he could do not to shift and go find the other woman. She'd done so much to her own family that he found it hard to believe that she was part of the Warmer family. There was no doubt that she had a few screws loose, but he'd not say that to Cass. She was hurting badly enough.

Opening his eyes, not sure when he'd fallen asleep, Cass was still in his arms, but his brother Yanick was in the room. Asking him through their link how long he'd been there, he said it had only been a couple of minutes. Then he asked him what he could do for him.

"I have three of those projects that you asked me to

look into. One of them is going to be a bust. There aren't any volunteers who work at the hospital that are under the age of seventy. While they more than likely could do the job, I don't know that many of them would want to go around delivering meals to people, too. Who suggested that?"

"The hospital administrator. He said it would cut down on the need for trained task assistants who get paid to do that." Yanick said it figured. "I didn't think it would work either. There isn't a lot of the volunteers there in the first place, and like you said, they're not young people who have the energy to do that sort of thing. What about the other two jobs?"

"I'm still looking into the one about the greenhouse. I didn't think about growing the baskets filled with flowers locally. They spend upwards of three hundred dollars on each of the ones that are put on the street lights. Then they have to be watered, too. But I'm still looking into that one. I don't suppose you know who is in charge of that, do you?" He told him to try maintenance. They might be the ones doing it. "Good idea. The third one I'm just going to forget about. With your notes on it and the way I see the town thinking about buying them shirts to do themselves is a wash. The Twelfth Man Club is a bunch of cheerleaders and their moms running the place, and I don't know that they'd want to print-screen their own shirts. Too messy and time-consuming. It's a good plan and would save them a bunch of money, but I don't see anyone doing it." Cass woke up then.

"I'm sorry. I must have been a little tired. I've not been sleeping well." She smiled at his brother. "How are things going with you, Yanick? I heard you had a date with Missy Albert, and it didn't go the way she wanted it." His face got beet red, and now he had to know what happened.

"If not for you, she would have had enough *evidence* to make me have to marry her. I'm steering clear of her family from now on." He asked what had happened. "Cass gave me a heads up about Missy being pregnant by her boyfriend. I guess it's all over town that the boyfriend isn't stepping up to the plate. He doesn't trust that he's the only one that has been with her. Well, I wasn't going to either. Apparently, she's been telling everyone that she's going to have *my* child. I put a stop to that immediately. I said that I would sue if she kept running her mouth. I'd never heard the rumors, but Cass did and told me about them. Her dad wanted me to marry her so they could get their house 'fixed up real nice,' he said."

It wasn't funny, but he laughed. That sort of thing had been happening to them since before it was known they were wealthy. Being shifters made it so there was no chance for Missy to have Yanick's baby, but he did wonder at the evidence she had.

"Yanick had donated a bunch of clothing to

the clothing drive, and she'd gotten ahold of some of his clothing through that. It was iffy if the police were going to believe him or not." Cass stood up and hugged Yanick. "I always have your back. Remember that."

When she left them to their business, he sat up straighter in his chair. Yanick asked him if he'd been able to find out anything about Cindy, something that they'd all been calling her since the house incident. He told him what he'd told Cass, the entire thing.

"I can't imagine having a family member like that. I mean, Dad was bad, and he knocked us around a bit, but he never would have killed us, I don't think." Conri didn't say anything, but Yanick didn't seem to notice. "Well, I need to get going. I have some things I have to take care of at the house. I've decided to have all the carpets pulled up and replaced with hardwood floors. It's apparently the way to go nowadays. Also, before I forget to tell you, I've been out to the greenhouse a couple of times. It's coming along nicely, and the people working there seem to be having a good time."

"Good to know. Brew asked me about it the other day, and I'd not had a chance to get out there. Thanks. I don't suppose you've been to the car dealership? I heard good things going on out there since they figured out the commission checks and when they can get them." He said that he'd not but would go out there tomorrow. "Thanks. I want to be here when Howard and Elizabeth come home. They're not going to be in a good place when they talk to Howie."

After his brother left, he went to find Cass. She'd not eaten anything last night, and he was worried about her. This thing with her sister was taking its toll on everyone in town, too. But he was especially worried about the Warmer family and Cass.

"I was just going to have a cup of tea. Would you like some?" He told her that he'd love a cup. "Good. I've been thinking about us and wondering if you'd sleep with me tonight. Not today. I want to talk to my dad and mom when they get back. They're devastated, I would imagine. I know that I am. And we don't even have to have sex, but just sleeping on you earlier, I slept better than I have in a while. What do you think?"

He couldn't speak. His body was so ready for her that he didn't know if he could go on much longer, sleeping in his big bed all by himself. When he realized she was waiting for an answer, he sat up on the stool and tried to remember how to speak. Smiling at her, he told her that he was there for her for whatever she needed him for.

"So you're all right with sleeping next to me without sex." It wasn't a question, but he felt that he needed to answer her. "All throughout eternity, you don't care to have sex with me."

It was a trap. He didn't know how he'd tumbled down the path that was going to get him into trouble, but he was as sure as he could be that he was on the crest of a fall that was going to have him regretting opening his mouth. Finally, he decided on the truth.

"I would have sex with you on this table with the tea cups rattling around. Against the wall, the door, hell, even the floor. But not until you say that you want it. And I stand by that. If you want to just sleep with me through all eternity, then I'll figure out some way to make it happen for you. Forever." She looked at him like she didn't know him. "I told you before, if you want to have sex or make love with me, then you're going to have to tell me. I'll not force you into anything ever. I promise you that on the heart of my mother, you're safe with me."

"I see." She didn't move when the tea kettle began to scream the steam out of the little spout. She did, however, move the cups off the table and to the counter. When she turned her back to him, he decided that he could take in a deep breath, and it nearly killed him when he realized that she was in heat. As soon as she turned back to him, his breath caught in his throat. She was crying. "I don't know how to be sexy. Or how to start sex with someone. I've had it before, but it was more of a one-night stand that didn't mean anything to either of us. I don't want that with you."

"I don't either. And honey, if you were to be any more sexy than you are right now, I'd be a dead man. I swear to you, you're the most beautiful creature I've ever seen. And I love you with all that I am." She nodded, wiping at her tears. "Don't cry, honey. It breaks me down inside to see you crying over something that I've said or done to you. I'm so sorry that you don't feel like you're sexy. You are. So much so."

"Will you make love to me tonight? I know that's hours from now, but I really do want to be there for my mom and dad. Howie is coming over as well tonight. I'm thinking that by the time dinner rolls around, they're going to be going to bed. This sort of thing wears them out. You know, stress. Howie will be stressed too about Margaret and his son, but—I'm babbling. I do that when I'm nervous." He told her that he loved her. "I'm glad you didn't say that you loved me when I babble, or I'd be doing it all the time. You make me nervous."

"Why?" She told him. "I don't actually lift cars for fun, you know. I'm just this big because I'm the alpha. I do keep in shape. And as soon as the two of us bond or make love, you'll be stronger, too. Not like me, but you'll be able to handle yourself all the time, too."

"So, you're all right with sleeping with me tonight? I don't know how sexy I'll be after talking with my parents, but I want you in my bed." He told her he'd be there for her. "Good. Something epic to look forward to." She kissed him on the mouth and left him there. He'd not gotten any tea either.

Chapter 6

Howard was so depressed that he didn't think it could get any worse. His firstborn, his daughter, wanted him to kill his family and then allow the police to kill him for attention for her. It has always been about her, he'd only just realized, and he should have done something about it back when she was younger, he knew now.

"Dad, it's going to be fine. She's not going to get out." He looked at his son and wanted to cry all over again. "I'm trying to think of positive things about her, to be honest, and I can't get over the fact that she killed Maggie and Howard the third. Why would she do anything like that to me? I thought that we were close. I was no competition to her at all."

That was all it took for him to start to cry again. His grandson was gone because, according to Cynthia, he was in the way. An innocent child who hadn't even taken his first breath was gone because of his daughter. When Howie had come to sit with him, the two of them clung to one another, sobbing about the fairness of her getting to live while others around her had not.

Howie was grieving all over again for the loss

of something so profound as his son and wife. And there was nothing he could do about it. Just hold onto him like before, telling him that it was the will of some higher power than them that had made the decision to end the life of two of the people that he'd come to love. He thought that was better than saying that his bitch of a sister had done it and he was sorry.

None of them were doing well tonight. Elizabeth had gotten in touch with her doctor and told him she needed something to calm her nerves. He ended up leaving something for him, too. The stress wasn't good for his head. Howard got up from the couch and went in search of Conri. The man had a calming effect on him like he'd never felt before. He found him and Cass in the kitchen having tea.

"May I have some?" Conri said that he'd make it, and when he stood up to do so, he kissed Cass on the mouth. Usually, it bothered him when they would do that, but tonight, it was wonderful to see them enjoying each other like nothing was going on. "You have become the balm that I needed all day. I can't believe that it was only just this morning that I had a talk with Cynthia. It seems so long ago now. Like I've been grieving for what she's done all my life."

"I'm not saying that what she's done is all right, but you do know that you're giving her just what she wanted in telling you that." He asked Conri what he meant. "She's the center of your life right now. Getting the attention that she wants."

Howard sat there sipping his tea and thought about what Conri was saying. He was right, of course. If she were here now, she'd be loving that they're all thinking about her. Really making her a large part of their life right now. When he was given some cookies to go with his tea, he started to turn them away, but he thought once again about giving her attention. After taking three of them and eating them with his tea, he did feel better than he had before coming into the kitchen.

"It's hard not to think about what she's done, but I believe you're right in letting her ruin our day. We need to move on, think about how we're going to build a new house, not dwell on the fact that she's the one who blew up the house in the first place." He finished his tea. "Yes, you're right. We need to focus on the things we need to in order to not give her anything that she wants. Thank you, Conri. Thank you so very much."

When he went back to the living room, he asked Elizabeth if she wanted to take a ride with him. One of the houses that they'd looked at to build was right here in town. They could go there, have a look at it, and make a decision as to whether they like it or not. Then, perhaps, go out to the building site and try to imagine what the house was going to look like with the place they'd picked out on the ranch.

They'd decided not to build in the same place. The house was going to be more friendly to them in their golden age, with a one-floor plan that would keep them from having to climb stairs. He wasn't thinking of dying either. He and Elizabeth had decided that he had forever to live out the rest of his life with her. And damn the person who thought to take that away from them. She asked him if they could do it later, and he lifted her up off the couch and kissed her.

"No, we have to do this now. We're not going to talk about Cindy—what I've decided to call her today. We're not even going to think about her. Today is for making new memories and having fun. She's gone, done what she's done to us, and we're going to move on before we're nothing but a bag of old bones. Understand?"

She smiled at him. It was a watery smile, but he was going to take what he could get today. But tomorrow and all the tomorrows they had left, he was going to live each day like it was his last. Because it might well be for him.

The drive out to the house was quiet, but then, they weren't the type of people to chatter on about things. As soon as they got to the house, they decided that it wasn't for them. The blueprints showed a grand window in the front, and this house had it, too. But the sun glaring off the window had to have shades drawn, and he didn't think he'd like that. On their way to the ranch, they stopped and got some lunch at the Dari Q.

"I'm going to have me a hot chicken sammich. And some fries. Plus a milkshake. We're living for the day today, love. Get whatever you want. My treat." She laughed hard, and he squeezed her hand slightly. After she ordered the same thing, they sat on one of the benches and waited, enjoying the children coming up from the ball field after a game. "Did you win or lose?"

The boy and girl said that they'd both won their games. Feeling like he needed a little boost today, he offered to buy them lunch and ice cream. Well received, they laughed when the girl got herself two burgers and the boy only the one. It was a wonderful way to spend the afternoon.

"Howard, let's not build a house out there. I want to be in town. Closer to Conri and Cass." He had been thinking the same thing and told her that. "I want to be around people too. Coming here, this was a perfect idea. We could do this more often. Not just having lunch but going to ball games and hanging out with the kids. Remember when Cass was forever selling something? We could be one of the people who will buy those candy bars or wrapping paper and fund their trips to wherever. She cried just a little until their food was brought to them. Then she looked at him. "I don't know what I'm going to do."

"You'll be fine, my love." He had to look away a moment so he'd not join her crying, and they scared the kids. "You've no idea how much I'm going to miss you. How I'm going to...oh love, I'm going to miss you so much." He took out his hanky and blew his nose before he got out of hand. "Let's not talk about it today, love. I need today as much as you do." She nodded, her eyes full of tears, and when she reached for his hand, he took it. She was the best part of their marriage.

"Now, let's have our meal and then go and look for houses. I still want one floor, don't you?" They talked about anything and everything but his impending death. How they had to start over with everything. "One thing that I've learned over the years is getting really good towels if you want them to last as long as possible."

House hunting was hit or miss. They'd find one that they liked, but it was too far from where they wanted to be. Or they'd find one that was in the perfect spot, but the house wasn't for sale. They finally decided that they'd put an offer in on the house that was close to where they would be close to the kids, and while it wasn't perfect for them, it would serve as a good home for the future. The one without—no, he told himself, he wasn't going to think about leaving his family today.

It was late when they got home. There were sandwiches in the fridge they'd been told, the note even saying that they were going to cook out tomorrow night, and they got them two each and took them to their room. They honestly loved living here; they were on the first floor and had their family right here, but they didn't want to intrude on things going on between Conri and Cass. They were just newlyweds.

After Elizabeth was asleep, he got up and went to find his laptop. It had been at Conri's place, so it didn't suffer any damage. Pulling up an email to send to his attorney, he decided it was high time that he changed his will. After talking to his son, he was ready for what he'd been thinking about since Cass met Conri. He wanted to leave him part of his estate as well.

While he knew that he didn't need the money, the man had been saving all his life, and he'd had a very long one. He wanted some of his things to go to the man. He didn't have any treasures that he could hand down. However, he did have things that came from his heart that he wanted to say to him. Also, he wanted to leave Elizabeth in good hands. Knowing the other man as well as he thought that he could, he knew that even without asking, he'd be a good person for his

wife to lean on when the time came for him to die. That
was another thing that he only just then remembered.
He didn't want to linger in a vegetative state. When he
was gone, he wanted to be gone. He and Elizabeth had
talked about it, but he was worried that she'd not want
to pull the plug when the time was right.

Then there was the matter of Cindy. What to
do about her. He didn't want to even mention her, but
he had a friend who hadn't mentioned his son in his
will, and the son had sued the estate. It had made the
process drawn out for years and years. While the other
members of the family that he'd left things to — money
and stocks and bonds his business failed because there
was no one to run it. He didn't know if she'd get the
chance to sue the estate for a part, but he didn't want
to take the chance.

It took him four tries, but he finally got it right,
he thought. He mentioned how she'd taken their house
from them and other things that she'd destroyed in the
process. Then he went on to say that she'd been locked
up in the asylum for the rest of her life, and since it
was being handled by the state, he didn't want to have
anything to do with her. Not even when she died.

Going back to bed, he wrapped himself around
his wife. She was a comfort to him in ways that she'd
never understand, nor could he explain it to her. He
was going to miss her but hoped that when the time

came, she'd be brave. Elizabeth was the strongest person he knew, and he was ever so thankful that he'd gotten to share the last forty-six years with her.

~*~

Conri didn't know what to do when Cass came out of the bathroom. He loved her pajamas. They were white and had bright pink flamingos all over them. Even her slippers were the same bright pink color.

She climbed into bed with him, and he held her. She looked up at him from her back position and smiled. It didn't look happy, but something akin to fear on her face. He assured her that he'd never hurt her.

"I know that. I really do. But as I said before, I've had sex before, and while it was all right, I know that it's going to be nothing like it will be with you." He told her that he'd have to bite her and that she could bite him back. "I don't know about that. I don't know that I could bite anyone and draw blood. I'm assuming that's required of you."

"Yes. It's quite enjoyable from what I've heard." She smacked him on the chest, and he laughed. "I won't do it if you don't want, love. I'll just lick your throat and let you feel how good that feels. Trust me, it feels great. Tell me you'll do it for me."

"You're very needy. Or are you like this all the time?" He said just when he was about to make love to his mate. "And how many mates have you had over your long life?"

"You're the second one, but you mean so much more to me than she ever did. There had always been something so terribly off about her that I realize now that I never fully accepted her nor trusted her." She just stared at him. "She betrayed me with my father. They stole a great deal of money from not just myself but the pack as well. It was terrible."

"I'm so sorry. I didn't know." Conri told her that it was all right that he was finally over it all. "Are you sure that you're over her? And...that's why you didn't trust me at first. You never fully recovered from what she'd done to you. Do you trust me now?"

"I do. I love you like I never loved her. And once we bond, we'll have the life that we wanted and that I've never gotten before. I love you, Cass." He leaned down and kissed her on the mouth. "I will love you forever and a day."

Nuzzling her neck, he could feel her pulse there just below her ear. It was pounding so hard that when he paused for a moment, he could hear her blood racing through her veins. Hearing her sharp intake of breath had his teeth shifting and sharpening. So as not to cause her too much pain but allow her to lick his own throat, he paused a moment. Licking her again, feeling the pulse pounding against his tongue, Conri bit her there. His teeth sank into her muscle so hard that she cried out with it. Her release permeated the air around them. He made his way down her body, nipping and kissing her body as he went. Then he got to the apex of her thighs and inhaled deeply of her scent. Cass was so wet she told him that she was embarrassed by it.

"I need to taste you, Cass. I want to see if you taste as wonderful as you smell." He jerked the pants and panties off her, and she cried out again when he nipped at her thigh. "I want to feel you come down my throat."

Her body was responding to him before her mind could come up with a reason why this was a bad idea. And that was the way that he wanted it. Conri was between her legs, which he'd put on either side of his head before she could protest if she was ever going to. As soon as he pulled her clit into his mouth, she cried out his name and came. Never had anything made him feel this way about anyone else.

He ate her like he was never going to stop, which was just as well as he didn't plan on it. The more he took from her, the more she gave him, the more she got. Every time he bit down on her, she came crying out his name. Every time he slid his tongue into her sheath, he knew that she was going to come again and again. Her juices were soaking him. When he slid his fingers into her, she rode his hand, her hips coming up off the bed like he was fucking her, and he realized that she wanted him to.

"Come for me again. Come and let me drink from you again." She laid back, her body so taunt with need that when he sucked her clit into his mouth as he stretched her with his fingers, she bowed up off the bed and screamed. He never stopped taking her, even when he begged him to stop.

When he stood up over her, she could see that he'd released his cock. The thought of him taking her, his thick cock entering Cass, he knew that it was going to hurt. But instead of sliding into her like they both wanted, he fisted his cock until long streams of his precum fell onto her.

"I'm not going to take you the first time where I might well hurt you. I'm going to be soft and as gentle as I can be." He moaned when she reached for him. "Honey, you touch me, and it's going to be over right now. I want to come all over you. Have my cum spray all over your pretty pussy until you come again. Tell me you want it. Tell me, Cass, tell me you want me."

"Please." He leaned over her and took her mouth. She could feel the head of his cock just at her entrance. When he bowed back, lifting his head from her, he roared out as he filled her, his cock slamming into her until she screamed with the pain. Over and over, he took her hard, and she hurt. Hurt so badly that she wanted him to stop.

Conri dropped over her and held her. His cock was still inside of her, and he was afraid to move. He had no idea if she'd arouse him again so that he'd want to do it again, so he laid very still. When he lifted his head and looked down at her, she turned her face away.

"Look at me, please." She didn't, and he repeated her name. "Cass, look at me so I can see how badly I hurt you."

"I'm embarrassed if you want to know the truth. I've never been so wanton before ever. It felt so good, but I'm going to be sore too." She finally looked at him. "I loved that. Even the end where you came inside of me. And I swear to you that I could feel it, too. All of you as you came inside of me."

He moved gently inside of her, causing her to moan again. "I love you so much, Cass. I don't know what I'd do if not for you being with me right now." He held her to him.

Conri woke up holding onto Cass. Rolling to his back, taking her with him, he held her tightly to his chest while she slept on. Running his finger up and down her back, he told her how much he enjoyed making love to her while she slept. He felt like he'd been given the world and the sun, too, when she turned and kissed him on his chest. Holding her firmly, he asked her if she was all right.

"I am, actually. I feel better now that I've had a nap. I could sleep more if you don't mind." He said that he thought he could sleep as well and pulled the blanket up and over the two of them. After telling her that he could as well, the two of them snuggled down into the comforter and held onto each other.

It was nearly sunrise when he opened his eyes. Unlike before, he was alone in the big bed, but he didn't have to worry. She was just coming out of the bathroom in one of his shirts that hung to her thighs and hurried across the floor. As soon as she was in the bed, he pulled her close even though her body was cold and rubbed her back and arms. She'd gotten chilly while running to the bathroom.

"I have so much to do today. Mom and Dad want me to go and see this house they want to move into. I'd rather they just stay here, but I don't know how to make them believe that that's what I really want." He said to just tell them. "Mom thinks that we're still on some kind of honeymoon and don't want them around. I think we just proved that they don't need to be gone from here for us to have fun." She finally got up, and he did as well. "I think I need a long hot shower and then maybe another nap."

"I can talk to them if you want. I think that in the long run, it'll be better for your mom to live here when your dad dies. I'm sorry to bring that up, but most of his year is still out there, and they need to make arrangements. What are they going to do with the ranch if they're going to live in a house in town?" She told him what her mom had said to her, that they were going to leave it to him. "I would think that Howie would want it."

"He's never liked the horses. Never had anything to do with the ranch either. I think that he's planning on selling the house that he's in now because of the memories that are now associated with it. Like it's tainted now that he knows that Cynthia killed Margaret and his son." She turned on the water and stood waiting for it to warm up. "I can't say that I blame him. He has gone through a great deal since Cynthia confessed. I feel so sorry for him right now."

"I do as well. To find out after all this time that his wife was killed by his sister would be a terrible blow to his heart. I'm betting that it takes him longer to get over this than it did when they were first killed." She said she thought so as well. "Poor guy. I really do like him. Maybe we can get together soon and just have a brothers' night out with my brothers, too."

"That would be wonderful. He'd like that too." She got into the shower, and he joined her. No hankie panky, she told him, as she was still very sore, but he could scrub her back. Not only did he do that for her, but he also scrubbed her hair too. He loved the feeling of the rich silkiness of it as he rinsed it for her, too.

When she left, he sat in his office and started working on the pack things. There was plenty for him to do, but when Howie called him to ask a favor, he leapt at the chance to hang out with him.

"There is this house that I've been looking at before I settled on this one. Margaret never liked it, which, at the time, I could understand it. There are only two bedrooms. But this house is too large for me. I've had enough of trying to keep it up and also the lawn." He asked him the address of the house. After telling him, Conri laughed. "I own that. If you want to move into it just for something temporary, that's fine with me, too. Or forever. When I purchased it, it was part of a group of homes that I got from the city. It's been completely remodeled, and the yard has been cleaned up, but you can have it. If you have dinner with me and my brothers some night soon. We try to get together weekly, and I'd love for you to come with us."

"I would love that. What will your brothers think of me coming along?" He told him that they'd be upset that they didn't think of it before him. "Thanks, Conri. You have no idea how much I'd enjoy that with you guys."

"We'll go tonight. We've been working hard on things around here and deserve a break. Your sister is hanging out with your parents tonight, and we'll have some fun." He reached out to talk to his brothers and was thrilled that they were all able to make it. He told Howie. "We usually go to someplace where we can have a couple of beers. We don't normally drink as it doesn't have much effect on us, but we'll have some dinner and a couple of them."

He made plans with the younger man. After telling Cass what they were doing, she decided to have dinner with her own parents. It would be fun for them as well after looking at houses all day. After hanging up with her, he was surprised when she called him back a few seconds later.

"I've convinced them that they don't have to buy a home but can live with us. We're still going to keep looking in case they find something that they really want. I doubt it. They had a list of things that they want, and there aren't too many houses out there for the price they want to pay." He told her that he owned a lot of houses in town to let him know where they were, and they could have them if they wanted to live there. He'd even sign it over to the two of them if they wanted to go that route. "I'll get the list together, and we can look it over tonight. What a wonderful husband you've turned out to be. I'll let them know."

He laughed. "I'm trying my best to be about as wonderful as I can be. It's easy when you have the best wife in the world. And you are, too." She told him thanks and hung up. After getting ready, wearing a nice pair of jeans and a polo shirt, he wasn't the least bit surprised to find that his brothers were all dressed the same way as was Howie. The man did look beaten, however.

"I heard from the insurance company. They were notified by the police and my attorney that my wife was killed by my sister. I'm not sure why they have to exhume hers and Howard's bodies, but he said it could be a bigger payout. I'm not really worried about that. It was an accident before, and I don't know that that would change anything." He told him. "Yes, I suppose that could be called a homicide now. I didn't think about that. I should have. I can't believe it when I think about it that she killed them. Some days are worse than others when I get all depressed about it."

"I don't know how you're standing upright, Howie. I don't know how you're being so brave." He said he had to be for his parents. "That's as good a reason as any. I hurt for you and your family. Have you given any thought to what you're going to do with all the furniture that you have in the bigger house? Your parents are looking at homes too to purchase."

"Dad told me last night. He said that he wants to make sure that Mom is settled before he passes. It's hard to talk to him when he gets like that. Sharing information. All I want to do is for him to stop talking about it. It's coming faster than I'd like to think about."

"I understand that. I just met him and am hurting at his soon departure. I'm still waiting to hear from my king on making them immortal as well. Along with you." He said he didn't know if he wanted it just now. "I understand that too. You've had a lot to think over. A lot of changes that you weren't expecting.

When they got to the restaurant, his brothers were already there. They had a table made up for them in a private area of the place where they could talk about anything that they wanted and about as loud as they needed. And they were loud when they were all together, and that was what made them get along so well. They were big men with big ideas, his mom would say often about them. He was going to have to make time for her too soon.

Chapter 7

Kendrick had one more patient to go, and he was done for the week. And he was ready for it, too. This weekend, he was going to clean out his garage and get rid of some of the things he'd been harboring since he'd moved in. He hated to think about the dozen or so boxes that were still out there that he'd not unpacked since he'd moved in about ten to fifteen years ago. He figured that if whatever was in them he'd not been missing, then they were to be tossed out. He wanted to clear out the old in order to make room for the new. And by now, it might only be stuff that he had stored in a storage lot some time ago.

Moving every ten to fifteen years was something that he thought all of them did, with the exception of Conri. He had lived in the pack house now for about fifty years. For at least as long as it had been built anyway. It really did give them a fresh outlook and had them seem less stationary about their lives. He enjoyed it as a way to get everything fresh. He'd buy not just furniture to go with his new house but new everything, including towels and sheets. They probably needed to be changed out more often than that, but he never deviated from his plan, and that had been working out well for him. His brothers, too, he thought.

"Doctor Valley, a child is being brought in that has a rash on their arm. The mother is frantic about it. She just wants you to look at it to see if she needs to take him to the emergency department. I guess the wait there today is about six hours to be seen. She's trying to cut out the middle man, I think, in being there." He asked her if she was serious about the wait at the ER. "I am. Once in a while, I'll call over there and get an update in the event someone needs to be seen by you. Since I know they can get reports back quicker than you can, I'll sometimes send them directly to them. Not for just small boo-boos but larger things like cuts and such."

"I'll see them. You keep an eye on the ER for me, and we'll see if they could use some help. I'm off this weekend, and I had plans, but if they need help, I can certainly go there and see if I can help." She told him that she'd keep that in mind. Sally was a good receptionist, and he enjoyed working with her. "Let me know when they get here. Mr. Johnson is getting dressed and will be ready to go soon."

"I'll take care of him." She'd make him feel like his appointment was one that he'd been looking forward to all week, and he'd go out with a puffed-out chest. That was another thing he liked about her. She was very good with patients. "Oh, their names are Pirate. Jane and Willy Pirate. She's asked for an appointment to see you when you have time as a new patient. I guess they just moved here. Father is out of the picture, so you know."

He didn't need to know that, but it was he supposed good to know in case it came up for some reason. Sally wasn't a gossip, but she knew a great deal about people around town. Some of it was good, but most of it wasn't for the casual listener. When he said she knew a lot, she really knew the skeletons in everyone's closet, including his own. But as he thought to himself, she wasn't one to gossip about anyone.

Willy came in with his mom, Jane, about five minutes after five. He took the little boy back to the rooms while his mom filled out paperwork for insurance and such. He didn't bother with that part but was glad that Sally had a handle on all the companies and their insurance so that he would get paid when it was time. Setting Willy up on the table, he had a look at his arm.

"This is poison ivy. Do you have it anywhere else on your body?" Checking him out, he found that it wasn't just on his right arm but his left and on both his calves, too. There were small spots of it started on his back, and he found it on his cheek. It was time for the big guns and a shot. But he had to wait on his mom to see what she wanted him to do. When she entered the office, he thought she was far too young to have a little boy of Willy's age but didn't say anything to her. It wasn't any of his business, first of all, and secondly, Sally would more than likely know before anyone else what the family dynamics were.

He ended up giving the boy a shot and recommending some ointment for his more raw skin. Scratching it could cause an infection, and he didn't want that to happen to the little man. He certainly had been brave while giving him a shot of steroids and antibiotics and giving him a prescription for it for home.

It was nearing six when he finally got out of the office. Sally had left at five-thirty, telling him that she was going to the bank and post office. Good, one less thing that he had to do on his way home. Going to the Dari Q for dinner, he was surprised to find Howard there talking to a bunch of the ball players from some of the local teams. Getting his food, being invited to sit with the older-looking man, he asked him how he was feeling.

"I'm doing all right. Wearing out a little faster than I used to, but I suppose that is to be expected. Having this thing in my head, it's certainly messed up my plans for the future." He was sure it had and told him so. "I'm taking your advice, young man, and going to go to another doctor for a second opinion. Thank you for that. You said that you might well have someone in mind who could do it for me, right?"

"I do. Two doctors that I can recommend are only in Columbus at Ohio State Hospital, you could easily see. I'll call them and get you in earlier than I think they're seeing new patients." Howard said that he'd like that. "I'll call them tonight. They practice together, so it might be one or both of them that you get to see. They're the best in their fields of brain surgery."

"You have any opinions on how I look now as opposed to when I started coming around? I don't see you as much as I do your brothers, so I thought that I'd ask." Taking a bite of his sandwich, he looked at the man. "All you Valley men, you're good men and take questions seriously, don't you?"

"Yes, I know that we all do. Our dad would never answer questions when asked of him. It was like the old saying goes that it was like pulling teeth. In the end, we figured out that he couldn't lie to us, so in not answering, he got away with a lot of things that he shouldn't have." Howard said he'd heard that he wasn't a good man. "No, he wasn't. He was a terrible man, leader, and father. We're all glad that he's gone. I'm sure that makes us sound cold and heartless, but that's what we all feel towards him. My mom is only still alive because she pulled her claiming of him when she found out that he'd been stealing from the pack and even her. My mom is a full-blooded wolf, but my dad was human. Him being made alpha was only because she was such a good person."

"I didn't know that. You all are half-bloods, then?" He said that they had very few traits that made them look like half-blooded wolves and were, for the most part, full-blooded. "Good to know. Yes, sir, it's good to know about that. Not that it changes how I feel about you. You six are about the best thing that has happened to us and my little family."

"Thank you. We feel the same about you and your family, too. It's been great getting to know you all." Kendrick finished his dinner and watched Howard as he interacted with the boys and girls coming up to get some dinner as well. The games this time of year would be well past nine o'clock because the sun was still out and shining then. One of the boys asked him if he was going to be at their next game. "Yes. It's my turn tomorrow to be the doctor on site. I'm glad you mentioned it. I had completely forgotten about it. Thanks, Harley."

Now, he'd have to change his plans around. That didn't mean that he wasn't going to get anything done. It just meant that he was going to have to readjust his thinking on how much he was planning on getting done. He might well get the garage cleaned out, but nothing tossed out until he had more time. But it mattered little. He loved being the doctor on duty when they played games. It would mean that he would be there about twelve to fourteen hours, but he also got anything he wanted to eat and drink, as well as getting to see some really good games while he was at it.

"I might come down and keep you company. Elizabeth and Cass are going to go over plans for the houses we're going to be looking at. Conri said he owns a lot of the houses around where the pack house is, and so does his friend Brewster Smith. He is a nice man, and I just think the world of his wife. They're vampires, correct?" Kendrick said that they were but that Brew was about as old as they all were. "Yes, when I saw him talking to one of your brothers, he explained to me that he was an ancient. I did wonder how old he was."

"He's a good man. The land that the pack house and the pack land is all his. He kindly doesn't charge us anything to use the land, and we return the favor by keeping him and his family safe from people out looking to kill an ancient vampire and his mate." Howard, for some reason, thought that was funny being as powerful as the man seemed to be, but he told them that he had to sleep sometime during the day, and that was when he was vulnerable. "Yes, I guess I should have thought of that too. My pardon. I didn't mean to make fun of him. It just seemed funny for such a man."

Howard decided that he needed to get home but asked if he could join him at the fields tomorrow. Telling him it would be good to have someone around, they were going to meet up at eight at the field to start their day. He was actually looking forward to it more than he had been when he remembered he was going to be stuck all day at the ball fields.

Making his way home, Kendrick decided to get himself a case of water from the store and then pick up some lunch meat to make him a couple of sandwiches. He could only eat so many hot dogs before he'd be sick. This way, he wouldn't be drinking a great deal of their waters, too, they made the best money on. The pack, as a whole, donated several hundred cases of water to the park to be sold throughout the summer so that they could afford to pay for umpires as well as ball uniforms for the kids and coaches.

Since he had a landline like the others did, he checked his machine to see that he had three messages. One of them was from Doctor Chris Baldwin, one of the very doctors that he had been going to call on behalf of Howard. He was told to call him back so long as it was before ten and he did so after getting his waters put away and his other groceries.

He told Chris about Howard. He'd left a message

earlier this week in saying that he might call him for a second opinion. After sending him the records that he'd gotten from the other man's doctor, he told him what he knew. Which to be honest with his friend, he didn't know a great deal.

"I do know that he was given a year or less to live. But to be honest with you, Chris, I can't believe how good the man looks for being close to death's bed. It's been a couple of months since he got his diagnosis, and he looks more fit now than he did when I first met him." He asked him what he was doing to look so good. "I know that he's eating better simply because his wife wants him to be around longer. And since they've been staying with my brother and his new mate, he's been walking around the town more. I just saw him this evening when he asked me if he looked any different. I had to admit that he did look trimmer than he did before. And certainly has a healthy glow to his skin."

"I've cleared my morning for him on Wednesday. Tell him to be there at eight in the morning, and I'll do a thorough workup on him and his wife while she's there. I tend to find that when this sort of thing happens, the other partner gets poorly because they're stressing over every little thing." He told him how they'd both been under a great deal of stress of late, and nothing to do with the tumor. "I'll work them both up and feel better about it. Yes, tell him that we'll see what we can find about his tumor and go from there."

"I'll bring them there myself if that helps them get there on time. Not that I'd think they would be late, but I'll make sure they get there." Chris asked him how his practice was going and mentioned how he was going to be at the ball field tomorrow. "I miss those days when I could do something like that. I'm so busy with my practice nowadays—demand is taking its toll on me as well. But I did love being around the kids when it was my turn to be at the ball fields. You mostly sit around, but it's fun nonetheless."

"I'll be on for about fourteen hours and get all the food and drink I want. On the way home tonight, I picked up some lunch meat so I'd not have to eat my weight in hot dogs tomorrow and be sick for a week." They both laughed. "Thank you for seeing my friend, Chris. He's my brother Conri's father-in-law, so you're doing a favor for a lot of people."

"It's my pleasure. Anything for an old friend." Thinking how long it had been since he'd seen Chris, he was sort of ashamed to be asking for a favor for so long an absence from each other's life. He'd have to make up for that in the future.

After getting a shower and setting his alarm, he was ready for bed. He did call Howard and let him know about the appointment and told him that he would clear his day on Wednesday to go with him and his wife if he wanted. Of course, he wanted him there as support, and he was glad that he had suggested it. It was going to be a long day, but at least he'd be able to answer questions if they had any on the way home. Not that they'd have all that much information on the way back, but he'd be there for them if there was anything that came up.

~*~

Conri was ready to call it a day today, and it was only eight-thirty in the morning. It had been a long night before, and now it was running into his morning issues that had been going on at the pack land. All he'd wanted to do was to have some of the men and women who were a part of the pack go out to the ceremony area and mow and do some trimming, and they were making it sound like he was asking them to cut off their left nuts to do it for them all.

"I have to pay for gas, too?" Conri told the man once again that whatever he spent would be taken off his dues for the month. "But that's a month away, and I'm going to be putting out the money now. That's not fair at all."

"I'll give you twenty bucks to mow the lawn and not take anything off your dues." That wasn't want he wanted either. "Look, I could just order you to do it, Carl, but I'm willing to pay you to do something for the pack. It's up to you. Either do it and get paid now or have it taken from your dues."

"I guess I'll take the money now. But I don't think it's fair that I have to use my own mower. Why don't the pack just buy a mower? That would be even better." He told him how they'd done that once before and how it had been used by some of the pack so much for their own yards, it wasn't worth doing it again. Not and have a mower for everyone to use. "I remember that. It was sure nice having that rider when I had to mow my own lawn. You should really think about buying another one. I'd surely like that."

"I'm sure that you would. But I'm not, so mow the lawn out at the ceremony field and think of it as paying for the other mower that you and the others wore out when you didn't want to buy your own mower." He, of course, thought that was a bad idea and said as much. "Look, Carl, I'm having five of you mow the lawn on the same day. I could just have you do it and take it all afternoon. Do it, and stop bitching about having the pack paying to have a new mower."

"I still think it would be great to have one around all the time. Mine isn't going to last forever having to mow the—All right, I'm going." The low growl had him leaving the pack meeting hall faster than he'd come into the hall.

He was making a list of people who would be

responsible for the lawn when the phone at his desk rang. He was in no mood to take any calls, so when he answered it, he knew he was a bit short with the person on the other end of the line.

"What a way to answer the phone. I raised you better than that." Of course, it would be his mom. And she'd not understand what was going on at the office today. "What is going on there? Has someone dirtied up your day already?"

"You have no idea." He told her about his day so far. "Then the phone rang, and I insulted you. I'm sorry, Mom. I hadn't any intentions of taking anything out on anyone else today, but you can understand this."

"Your father would have bought the mower and still not had the field mowed. Then wonder why. You're a good leader, son." He thanked her. "The reason that I called was I've been trying to get in touch with your wife. She's been putting me off. I don't know that she likes me all that much."

"Her dad is ill, Mom. You know that. And they're in Columbus today, getting a second opinion on his brain tumor. I hope it goes well. They're going to be there just about all day." Mom said she'd forgotten about him being ill. "Yes, sometimes I do as well. He looks so good otherwise."

"He does. Oh my, I feel so bad now. I'd forgotten

about him dealing with all that. I should have been there for her. You tell her when you talk to her if she needs me, all she needs to do is to call me, and I'll be there for her." He told his mom that she could contact her. "I will when she returns. Poor thing. I just love her family to pieces, Conri. You got yourself a good mate in her."

"I agree. She's been helping me with the pack stuff lately, too. She's the one who suggested that I get some of the members to mow the lawn out there. Except for the bitching today, I think it's going to work out well." She asked about other projects. "She's hired a firm to go over the books. She told me that she didn't think everyone was paying their dues on time, and most of them weren't paying them at all. We do have a few, very few, who pay by the year. I mean, it's not all that much to pay. But I believe she's right. Dues aren't being paid. And the ones that aren't are the first ones in line when we have something to give away to the groups."

"I don't believe I've paid mine now that I think about it." Conri told her that she didn't have to because she was the mother of the alpha. "Well, that's nice. Thank you for that. Do your brothers pay theirs?"

"No, they work for the pack in different ways, and that's why. When I need them, they'll run around gathering things up or checking things out for me.

Also, Kendrick is my second, though he doesn't care for the job. With him being a doctor, it's hard on him to go with me and knock a few heads around. He told me that he ends up having to take care of them once he's knocked them around." Mom laughed just as he had hoped that she would. "I'm thinking that I need to get one of the others signed up on it. Rette said he'd do it. I guess he's got all his things ready for his art show now, and he has some free time. But once he gets started again, it'll be difficult to pull him away."

"I have a hard enough time getting them to pay me any mind when they're in the fight or flight mode. I didn't realize that they had another show coming up. I need to get with them on a calendar so that I can keep up." He didn't know what to say about that, so he didn't. But his mom wasn't finished talking yet. "I called you to get in touch with Cass. I've done that already. I guess I should let you get back to work. I do miss having you boys around more often. I don't suppose you'd like to have lunch with your poor old mother today, would you?"

"I'd love that. I was going to get with Yanick, but he can join you and me if he behaves himself. When he's bored, he tends to get a little out of hand." She said that she would love that. "Well, it's about noon now. Do you want me to pick you up and bring you into town, or you drive yourself?"

"Pick me up. Oh, this is wonderful. I get to have a nice lunch with two of my boys." He was going to have to make more time with his mom if she was this excited about having lunch with him. All of them needed to do it more often. "I'll meet you in front of the house. I've got myself a grocery list too going on, and I'll just walk home with those little bits of things."

"I'll bring you back home. There is nothing on my desk that has to be done right away." There were actually ten things on his desk that needed his attention today, but his mom was very important to him. Getting his suit jacket—wearing a suit to work at the pack meeting house was something that he'd been doing since taking over—he made his way to the door while reaching for his brother.

"We have to make more time for her." Yanick beat him to saying it. *"Yesterday, when I was in town, I saw her talking to herself. Wondering where her boys were when she needed them. I was going to suggest we meet with her all together at least once a week and then by ourselves on another day. It'll be good for her. And us."*

"Maybe we can convince her to do Sunday dinners again. Those were so nice when we had them. We could all get together and talk." Yanick agreed with him. *"Also, you might not have thought of this, but we really need to get together for Christmas this year. Find out what we're going to be doing. In the last few years, we've done nothing but*

pack stuff, and I miss having a tree up."

"You're only saying that because you have a mate. And possibly children soon. So when are you going to make me an uncle? Soon, I hope. I'd love to see a little version of Cass running around." He thought that he would as well. *"I'm hoping you're going to be making an announcement soon. Or even at Christmas. That would be epic, big brother."*

"I don't have any announcements as yet, but I won't let you know when I do." They both laughed. *"I'm about to pick up Mom. I hope you're at least almost to the restaurant."*

"I'm there now making reservations for the four of us. Rette was in town, so I invited him too. You think Mom will care?" Conri told his brother that she would love it. *"All right. I'm getting her now. I'll see you in a few minutes.*

His mom was so excited that he felt twice as bad about not taking her out more often. Just because they all had jobs, they shouldn't be neglecting their mother. He'd hate it if his own kids, whenever he had them, did the same to him.

Not only were Yanick and Rette at the restaurant but so were Lamar and Yuri. Kendrick sent his best wishes to their mom as he was still in Columbus with the Warmer family, but having the five of them together, his mom couldn't have been happier. At one point, she did cry a little, her love for them shining through her tears, she told them. He was just glad that she'd called him today so that he could spend some time with her.

Lunch was a lot longer than he thought it would be. It was nearly three when they started off to the grocery store to pick up her few things. Never once did he allow himself to look at his watch, and he noticed that his brothers hadn't either. When they were finished, he asked if they would meet with him and Mom once a week so that she'd not feel so bad about them not coming around. They all agreed that they'd love to have a nice meal with them once a week. Or more, as it turned out.

There were a few people in the grocery store that spoke to his mom. She always made sure to tell them that they'd all just had lunch together and that they were going to pick her up to join them once a week. He felt like a heel when a couple of the women told her that it was about time, but mom ignored them in favor of being proud about having him shopping with her. He even pushed the cart around for her while she gathered up things that he was sure were at home in the cabinets.

By the time he got her home and the things brought into the house, he was sure that he felt better than he had even a few days ago. Something about having someone proud of you made you feel like you could take on just about anything. He realized, too, that at some point, his headache from earlier was gone, and he wasn't grinding his teeth so much. Yes, there was a lot to be said at having lunch with your mom, he thought.

Getting back to his office at five-thirty, he'd heard from Cass twice and Kendrick once. They'd have the test results in a few days, but things didn't look as badly as they were told.

"The tumor hasn't grown at all since the first cat scan. And not only that but in a few places, it looks as if it's shrunk in size a little. Right now, I'll take a quarter of an inch over it growing that much." He said that he was glad for them all. *"Dad is trying hard not to get his hopes up, but you can see it in his eyes that he's excited about the extra people looking into it."*

"I bet that he is. I know that he sounded excited about it when I spoke to him last night." She was telling him about the doctors being so nice when he was packing up to leave for the day. Everything on his desk would be there tomorrow, he thought. Today had been totally worth being behind another day. *"I love you so much, Cass. I'll see you when you get home."*

Chapter 8

Roger Went stood on the stoop of his favorite alpha's home and waited for him to come and allow him in. It was later than he expected to be showing up, but he knew that if they were all in their beds, they'd welcome him with open arms and big hearts. He so loved this family.

"Your lordship." He couldn't catch Conri fast enough before he was down on his back with his belly and throat exposed. "To what do we owe this honor?"

"Get up, man. Christ, with people doing that all the time, you'd think I was some sort of monster. Get up, Conri." He finally got the man to stand, but it was a moot point. His brothers were in the house as well, and he'd swear they dropped quicker than their brother did. The only person who didn't was a young woman with such beauty that he was ready to swear to her himself. "You must be Cassidy Warmer." She corrected him. "Sorry, yes, I heard that you had married. You're more beautiful than I heard."

"If you don't do whatever it is to get them up, I'm going to make it so you have to bow before everyone because you'll be broken." He laughed and told her that he tried his best not to have them do it, but it was something in their DNA that made it so. "I don't care. They look ready to die on this mountain, and I'm not ready to lose any of my family members just yet. Have you come here about my family?"

"I have indeed. Are they around, too?" She told him that they were just getting ready to sit down to dinner. Then she asked him if he'd like to join them. "I would. Thank you very much. I'm assuming that Ethel Valley is around, too?"

"I am. What brings you here…never mind. I remember. You certainly took your time in getting here. He's already heard from a second doctor, and the news hasn't been given to us yet. So this might be all for naught." Roger said that he'd still like to offer immortality to them if they wish it. "That will be up to them in whether they wanted it or not. I'm thinking they will, if only to be here when the children come. But that's not up to me."

Dinner was delightful. He got to meet the Warmer family and enjoyed the father a great deal. Another beautiful woman added to their family was in Elizabeth. She treated him much the same way that Ethel did in that she seemed to have no respect for him at all. Which he supposed was all right for now. After dinner, they retired to the living room, and he could already see the touches that Cass had made to the room by simply being around. Getting down to business, he took Howard's hands into his very much larger ones.

"How frank would you like me to be, Howard? I mean, I could ask you questions, but I do believe I know the answers to them." The man looked around the room and then back at him. His small yes was all he needed to tell the room it was much too late for him to help the older man. "You've been blacking out, haven't you? Sometimes, you will wake in a different area than you remember being in and have no idea how you got there."

"Yes. Sometimes, it is only for a few minutes, but now it's more like hours will be lost, and I haven't any idea if I've walked or driven myself to that point. Also, I'm assuming that you know about the memory loss, too." He said that he did. That his mind was a jumble of half ideas and memories. "I have no trouble remembering things from long ago, but daily memories are something that I've lost. And it's embarrassing." He looked around at his wife, then back at him again. "You can't help me, can you?"

"No. The tumor is shrinking. You're getting better. Tell him that, Howard. Tell him that you're getting better." His wife came and sat on the floor in front of her husband. "Tell him that it's fine and that you want to be here forever."

"I don't want to be here forever like I am right now. And we both know that I'm not getting better. We knew that as soon as the doctor told me that the tumor had shrunk." They all looked confused. "If he gives me immortality, I have a feeling that it's not going to help me as much as make me suffer for the rest of my life. Suffer with memory losses, big holes in my day where I can't remember what I was doing. That's it, isn't it? I would be just as I am right now, and you won't be able to fix that."

"You're correct. And it's not only the memories and black holes but the loss of appetite, too. You'll continue to lose weight simply because your brain no longer works like it did before. And while the tumor will no longer kill you, it will continue to incapacitate you until you are little more than a shell of a man. The damage has been done, and it is far more than I can fix even with my considerable magic." Cass told him that the doctors had hopes of him living longer. "I'm sure that they did. Giving him another six months to a year for him to continue on the path that he's on right now. There is no hope for him. And I'm sure if you were to think about what they said, they said they could prolong his life, not save it."

"He did say that." Kendrick was a good man, too, one that he'd come to depend on when he had medical questions that he might need answers to.

"Chris said that he could prolong his life, Cass, but he never mentioned saving it. I believe in my heart of hearts that he's going to tell you when he talks to you that the tumor has done its damage to the part of the brain where the shrinkage is. There is nothing left of that part of the brain for it to live off of."

"You're saying that the tumor is sucking his life away one part of his brain at a time." Kendrick told Elizabeth that was correct. "So we're no better off than we were before."

"No, that's not true. You will have a bit longer with him. Instead of the year that the other doctor gave you, you might have as much as two years. Will his life be productive and free of pain? No, it won't. He's going to pay for the extra time, and more of his memories will fade, and his blacking out or even becoming someone that is different than he is right now. There is no telling what will happen to him. This is a large tumor, and it's gone too long for anyone to be able to predict what's going to happen." Cass asked if immortality would make it better. "No. I'm sorry to say it will just make him worse for a lot longer. He'll suffer in ways that we won't understand until he gets there."

"I don't want him to die." No one said anything to Elizabeth's outburst. "Can't you do something? Is there anything that I can give you that will make him live out the rest of his days in peace and quiet with me?" No one said a word, but Conri got up and pulled the elderly woman from the floor. "Can you help him, Conri?"

"I wish that I could. But I promise you with all my heart that I'll make sure that his final days are pain-free. I'll hire round-the-clock staff to see to his every need. Then, when he passes, I'll take care that you never have another worry so long as you live. Cass and I will care for you so that—"

"I can't go on without him. I don't want to live without my husband by my side. Can't you understand that? He's all that I ever wanted in life, and now something is taking him away from me." When she collapsed in his arms, Conri stood there holding onto her as she sobbed her heart out. It touched him, too, the way that he comforted her with dignity and respect. Finally, when she seemed to cry herself out, he led her to the couch and sat her down next to her daughter. Cass and other members in the room were crying a great deal now as well.

Wiping at his eyes, he said that he could take away some of the pain but not all of it. It was considerable, too, the man was dealing with. It was a small wonder that he was even up and about. He could taste it on him.

"I want to die on my own terms. I need to die the way that I want to. With my family by my side when I take my last breath." Roger nodded, his own heart breaking for the man and his family. "I've already decided that I'm going to turn down the extra treatments that will be offered to me. The pain now is about as unbearable as I've ever dealt with."

"Dad, why didn't you say anything to us? We could have made things better for you. We certainly wouldn't have dragged you all the way to Columbus to get those extra tests. Were they that bad for you?" He nodded at his son. "Then I don't understand why you went through with it."

"Because it gave us all a little bit of hope. The pain was worth it to see that small glimmer of hope on all your faces." He turned to face the room. "I'm old and beaten. If I were to die tonight, I'd feel blessed that I got to see all my children today. Got to spend time with my friends and family. Would I do it again, go through all that prodding and poking? I would, just for you all."

Roger felt like he should leave but couldn't without causing a scene. So he sat on the couch with Conri and Cass, thinking about how much he wished he'd had better news. Something more than he wasn't able to help the man when, of all the people he knew, this man deserved it more than anyone else he'd been able to help.

"Will you make me immortal?" He was surprised

by the request from the son, Howie. "I'd like to live out an eternity with my sister if no one else. We've missed a great many years she and I, and I would like to be around."

Roger said that he could do that, and after taking his hand into his, it was done. The man looked shaken, but he went to his mother and sat on the floor in front of her. Whatever he was going to say, it was going to make the entire room sit up a little higher on their seats.

"I won't try and convince you to live with us. I know, we both know how much Dad means to you, and I won't ask you to do that. But I will ask you not to die soon. I have missed time with you and Dad as well. I need you in my life for whatever time we have left. The same with Dad. I want to be there with the two of you until the time is gone." He kissed the back of her hands as he continued. "Dad will say the same thing, I'm betting. You be here to gather up more memories and stories to tell him when you cross over to be with him. Children may not come from me again, but you know that Conri and Cass will have a houseful. The way they look at each other, I'm surprised they haven't told us yet that Cass is pregnant."

"You looked at Margaret the same way, too." He kissed his mom again. "I can't live without him, son. You two have your lives, but I don't want to be here without him. While I understand what you're asking me to do, I just don't know that I can do that."

"Yes, you can, Bethy, my dear. Yes, you can do that and more. I like the idea of you having this extra time to live here without me pestering you into things all the time. You store up those memories, and you bring them back to me. Tell me stories like only you can do for me." Elizabeth cried and said she didn't want to. "You have to do it for me, love. You need to do it for the children. As they said, they've missed time with us, and I believe that they'll be there for you forever." He went to her then and pulled her into his arms. "I have loved you since the first time I saw you coming out of that house on Main Street. Do you remember that? You were going on a date with another young man, and I tricked him into leaving you at that bar. I've always said that he must not have wanted to be around you if he was that easy. But I won that night and every day since then. Because I got you."

"You told him that his girlfriend was looking for him. He dropped me like a hot potato." Elizabeth laughed again as she picked up the story from Howard. "I do believe that the two of them married and divorced before we even had our first anniversary. You were the best thing that happened to me."

"You got that right. You've been my number-one girl since then. I love you, Bethy, my dear. And I will love you until you're by my side once again. Stay with them. Please? For me?" She asked him if he was planning on dying tonight. "No, I'm not planning on anything, but I just don't want to waste time anymore. We're going to live out what time we have left, like it's the last day. I love you. So very much."

"And I love you, too." She hugged him, still sobbing about him not being with her when he passed away. Roger thought that she was taking this a great deal better than he would have had this been his wife and family surrounding him. "I'll stay and try to make memories. I'm not going to even try and make you understand how much I'm going to miss you. But I do want to be able to see grandchildren. All right."

The rest of the evening was spent talking about family. There was a great deal that he didn't know and a lot more than he'd only heard little bits about. It made him sorry that he wasn't spending more time with his own kids. It wasn't as if he didn't have time, but he'd just kept working until they didn't bother asking for him to come and spend time with him. Roger decided he was going to take care of that as soon as he got home. Making time with family was something everyone should be doing, not just when they knew one of them was going to die soon.

~*~

Howard was exhausted, but he didn't feel the pain

like he'd been feeling the last few weeks. He knew that Roger had given him a bit of magic to help him along, and he was grateful for it. After taking his shower, he was ready for bed around midnight. Elizabeth had been in bed for about an hour now, and he went to their room to look in on her.

Sitting next to the bed in the room's only chair, he moved a lock of hair from her face so that he had a clear view of the face that he'd come to love all his life. Leaning back in the chair, he thought of all the things that had made him happy over the years. Seeing Elizabeth heavy with his children had been the most special of all his memories.

"I've made some changes to my will, love. It will benefit all of you when the time is right. I'm leaving the horse farm and all the land to Conri. Not that he thinks of it like he's beholding to the great vampire, but a pack needs their own land, I believe. He's been such a good man to all of us that I hate leaving him with the task too of taking care of Cindy. No matter what we say about writing her out of our lives, she is still our daughter, and I couldn't do that even if I wasn't sick with this damned tumor."

He thought of the things that he'd left the pack and the man who runs it. It made him think of his own beautiful daughter, Cass, and how much she seemed to love the big wolf. Smiling to himself, he thought of what his son said about them having a houseful of children by the way they looked at one another.

"I know that they don't need it, but I've set aside some money for their children to have a bit of a nest egg. And children that Howie might have, too. I don't think he'll mourn too much longer. He sees his sister's happiness, and I'm betting that he wants that for himself, too, before too much longer." He thought about the memories that she'd bring with her when she came to be with him and hoped that was true. That they could sit and talk about their family like he'd never left them. "I want to go now, love. I hate waiting daily for the pain to hit me so badly that it takes my breath away. I don't like not remembering things like names and people. It frustrates me so much that it makes me angry. I don't like that feeling either, just so you know."

When Elizabeth sighed heavily in her sleep and rolled to her back. He could see her face fully now and thought she was just as beautiful tonight as she was when they met all those years ago. She could still make his heart skip a few beats when she smiled like she was doing now.

"I know that I said I was ready to depart this life, and I am. But I'm hoping for just one more day with you. A day that we can hash out what you're going to be doing with the rest of your life. I want you to be happy, love. I want you to be able to hold our grandchildren and love on them. I want everything that I can't do now for you to do for me. Tell them… tell them every day that I would have loved them to pieces. Take them to my gravesite and tell them stories about me so that they know me." He thought about that. "No, don't do that. You can tell them stories when they ask, but don't bore them to death with daily stories about me. They'll get enough of me from all you telling them little stories. And don't take them to the grave. I don't want children there when they should be out and full of life in a yard someplace."

He looked out the window when he thought about how much he was going to miss, and it made him sad. Too sad to talk to his wife right then. While he allowed the tears to flow down his cheeks, he wondered if it would be painful when he died. Would the tumor hurt him more in the end and found himself to be a little frightened about that.

Looking at his wonderful wife, he could see the frowns that were marring her beautiful face and knew that he was the cause of it. Touching his finger to the slight marring, he told her that he loved her.

He must have dozed off in the chair because he was suddenly wide awake. Getting up, stumbling a little to the bathroom, he wondered if he'd been in here already as the toilet was running. Going back to the bed, he felt a wave of something roll over him, and he had to hold onto the dresser until he had his balance back.

It took him several tries to get back to the bed. Twice, he nearly fell when he released the dresser, and then he almost tripped up when he realized that he'd lost one of his slippers at some point. Getting into the bed, finally, he was glad for the size of the thing so that he'd not disturb Elizabeth with him trying to get the covers right and over him.

Lying there, he thought about the way he was feeling and was afraid. Afraid that this was the time and he wasn't going to get to talk to his wife or family again. Crying a little, he tried to remember the name of the young man who had taken them in and couldn't. It hurt his heart that he couldn't remember his son's name either.

"You'll be just fine." He looked over at his wife. "You'll be just fine if you want to go. I know that you're hurting."

He sobbed loudly and took her hand to his heart. Telling her how he was feeling again, he couldn't remember if he'd been up and about just now, and she told him that it didn't matter. That she had him now and that he could go to sleep if he wanted.

"But I might not wake up." She seemed to understand that as well and laid her head on his chest just over his heart. "I love you, Bethy love. With all that I am. I'm going to miss you so much."

"Shhhh. I have you. Close your eyes and tell me a story. The one where you tricked Dominic into leaving me at the party by myself." He said he didn't know who that was. "It's all right. I'm going to tell you one then. It's about this man who brought me roses all the time when he thought I could use a pick me up. How chocolates would just show up in the house when I've had a bad day." She patted his chest, and he nearly panicked when he couldn't remember who she was or why she was with him. "I have you, Howard. I want you to do what you need to do. Just close your eyes and think of me. All right?

"Yes, all right." It didn't seem important that he told her that he didn't know where he was nor who she was. Just closing his eyes, he could feel her breath on his chest, and it made him feel like he could take on the world. When he started to feel heavy, his body being weighted down with something akin to a weight being settled over him, he no longer felt panicky but calm for the first time in what seemed forever. "I love you and that you're here with me."

The weight was almost nearly taking his breath away, and he didn't seem to mind that. His head didn't hurt, but why he cared, he didn't understand. All he knew was that someone was with him at this time, and he didn't feel alone any longer. He felt...he had peace in his heart for whatever was going on, and his breath felt lighter like he didn't need to breathe anymore and didn't. The last thing that he felt, or even thought of before he faded away, was that he should know the woman in the bed with him, but it was too much. Fading, or whatever it was called, was taking everything away from him.

~*~

Cass held onto her mother's hand while the medics that had come with the ambulance had worked to save her father. He'd been gone since two mom had told her, and she hadn't been ready to let him go. She understood that more than she could explain to her mother how much she really did understand.

It was now six-thirty, and she'd been able to say her goodbyes too. Howie had been here at four, and he, too, got to go and sit with Dad for a time while they all waited. Her dad was gone. Her hero wasn't going to be around for her anymore. It didn't bother her as much as it might have if not for the calmness of her mother right now.

"We talked for a little while. I could hear him talking to me as well when he thought that I was asleep. Then I saw him getting up and wandering around the room like a caged animal, and I realized that he didn't know what was going on. I didn't want that for him, not if I could do something about it." Cass asked her if she'd let him go. "Yes. I told him that I had him, and he seemed to believe me, so I held him until I got up to talk to you."

"Did he have any pain, Mom?" She said that he hadn't. His heart just faded quietly away until he was gone. "That's all we could ask for him to go peacefully."

"Yes. I realized something else, too. I was being selfish about wanting him to live out that year when he was in so much pain. Your father was a proud man, and forgetting things like he'd been doing would have embarrassed him." Cass nodded and held hands with Conri, who had been there for all of them. "I told them they were wasting their time with trying to revive him. But they continue on doing it."

"They'll stop soon." Again, a calmness rolled over her. "Dad went out like he wanted with his family near him and in his own bed. I love that. He's at peace and no longer hurting like he was either."

Calling the police had been done by Conri. And only when they'd all had their time to say goodbye to him. There was some discussion about telling Cynthia, but that all went to the wayside while they talked about Dad and his dying the way that he had.

She would go and tell her and make sure that she was locked up well, but that would be the last time for a while. When her mother passed, she would go there again to tell her. It was important to her to make sure that she wasn't out of the loop, though she wasn't a good person. She did deserve to know when her parents were gone. And when the time came for Cynthia to take her last breath, she'd be notified, and that would be the end of her visits to the asylum.

"Your father had made sure that his wishes were known before the will was to be read. Sometimes, people forget that if they make arrangements in their will, the service will be delayed, or things might not be known until the reading of the will. But your father had everything arranged." Calling the funeral director had been her job, and she didn't feel the kind of grief that she thought she should. "He was a good man and well-loved by the townspeople."

"I know that. He was a great father, too. I'm going to miss him." The man, if he'd given her his name she, didn't remember it. "I'll be down with his suit in a couple of hours. The house is full right now. Is about noon all right with you?"

"I have everything that I need. He dropped off his suit the other day when he was in town. I have that and the other things that he wished to have with him when he passed. Some pictures and a good book he said that he'd not had a chance to read yet." She laughed, and it made her feel good. "Your father was a character too."

"Yes, I can see him doing that. Having time while waiting on my mom, I'm betting that he said about it." She was told that was exactly what he said. He'd have plenty of time to read the books that he'd not been able to.

"He told me that he hoped that heaven had a good library. That would be something that he missed, too." After getting off the phone with the man, she sat with her mom on the couch in their living room. She told her what dad had said about a good book going to be what kept him from being bored. And just like she hoped, her mom laughed and hard. Howie said he had one for him that he was going to slip into the casket as well. As well as a few pictures that he could take with him.

"I hope he gets to see Howard and Margaret too." Howie hugged her when she stood up. "You're the best sister in the world. I'm going to be looking forward to spending the rest of eternity with you by my side, little sister."

She was going to look forward to spending some time with him and Mom too, while she had her here. Knowing that everything had been taken care of by her dad surely did make her feel like he was getting whatever he wanted. Christ, she was going to miss her daddy.

Chapter 9

Conri decided to go with Cass to see her sister. It wasn't going to be easy on her, but he'd be there for her in the event it got out of hand. And if she got out of hand, he'd shift and kill her. No bones about it. He was about as finished with the other woman as he had been with his dad towards the end of his life.

The funeral had been lovely. There had been so many people showing up at the first showing that they'd had to add an additional day of viewing to accommodate the people that came by. Then, the reception at their home was larger than he could have imagined. Everyone coming, however, only had great things to say about the older man. Stories about how he'd been there when he was needed. How he'd been known to go to the school and help hand out books when needed and was a part of the mentorship at the high school. There were many stories like that one that cheered Elizabeth up when she heard them.

Then, there had been the reading of the will. He knew that Howard was going to leave him something he'd just not known what it was. But to leave him the insurance checks to rebuild the house and the ranch was something he was sure that he should have left to his son. He was to use it as pack land, and there were no restrictions on the land either. It was for him to use or not the way he wanted. And he wanted to make it the best pack land there was around.

But Howie said it was nothing that he wanted there. That his sister had tainted not just the ranch but the land that went with it. Conri'd not known that Howie's wife had been killed on the ranch when she lost their child. Now, here he was, the owner of a large estate with money to spend on it to bring it up to par. He didn't know if he should be grateful or pissed off at the man when he thought about it.

Now, here he was, driving to the asylum to see his daughter and tell her that her dad was dead and that he'd left her nothing in the will but for her to be buried at the place where she was hopefully going to spend the rest of her days at. He hoped so as well. He didn't want to have to kill her, and it would come to that if she were to get out again. And he'd have no regrets about it, either.

"Are you going in with me?" He told Cass that he was planning on it. "I heard from the doctor, and he said that Cynthia is in a state of limbo all the time. I'm not sure what that means, but I'm willing to bet that she's not going to be able to have much in the way to say to us. I'm thinking that they're keeping her doped up all the time to keep her out of trouble. Are you going in with me?"

She'd been asking him that same question several times over the last few hours, and each time, he told her that he was. He didn't know if she was reassuring herself or what, but he wasn't going to leave her alone when she seemed to be in this sort of state of unknowing. He'd do it himself if he thought it would make her feel better.

The building was imposing looking. There was nothing but a small sign in the front of the building to tell what it was and how long it had been there. He had an idea that people in town drove by this place several times a week and never thought of what could be behind the doors nor the kind of people that might be in some of the rooms. He knew that he'd have a hard time just thinking of it as anything but a home for people who needed extra care and help. And sometimes guards that would keep others safe that were within the doors.

"We're here to see Cynthia Smith." Conri had forgotten about that, too. That Cindy went by an anonymous name here so no one could track her down. Why they'd want to do that was beyond him, but then he didn't have to deal with this sort of thing all that often, so he'd know the ins and outs of a stay in one of these places. Once it was established which Cynthia Smith they were seeing, they were given badges and a long list of rules that they had to follow for their safety.

They couldn't touch the patient. He thought that was a good rule. Nor were they to agitate her in any way. Cindy was forever agitated, so he didn't know how that was supposed to work. There were other things, too. No outside food or drinks. No clothing that hadn't been approved by the doctor. They couldn't leave flowers or other things in the room either. Nothing sweet nor sugary was to be given to the patient. Don't unstrap the patient. Don't sit close to the patient any closer than four feet.

Some of the rules he thought were saying the same thing. But he wasn't going to do any of the things on the list, so it didn't bother him in the least bit to know that he wasn't going to give her any candy or fruits. When they were taken to her room, a guard would be with them for their safety. They went into a large room that looked like any other bedroom he'd ever been in. With the exception of the long cot in the middle of the room with a small figure in it chained to the bed.

He'd never realized how small Cindy was until then. She always seemed larger than life because of the way she acted all the time. She had on a gown that looked like all the other gowns in the place, but hers was stained and dirty. He thought that they should have cleaned her up after her breakfast, but he didn't know how that worked, so he kept his mouth shut.

"Cynthia, you have visitors." The guard gave a little shake to the figure in the bed. When she stirred and looked up at them, he got a look at Cindy's face. Christ, she'd aged twenty years in the few weeks she'd been here. "Come on, Cynthia, you have some people here that want to see you. Come on now, get up."

She was sat up in the bed, but it did nothing to improve her looks. Her hair looked like a rat's nest had taken up residence. Her nails, while short, were filthy and brown. He looked at the guard when he said he'd be outside and realized that he was loving the way they were shocked about how she looked.

"Get her cleaned up. Christ man, when was the last time someone combed her hair." He told him that they didn't have time for pampering. "It's just human decency to clean her up after she's eaten. And when was the last time she had a shower?"

"Like I said, we don't have time for pampering people like her." He asked him what that meant. "Killers. She'll get one when someone has time."

Against his better judgment, he grabbed the man by his shirt and tossed him against the wall. When it looked as if he was going to hit him, Conri let go a little of his wolf and told him to get her doctor. He didn't think that he was going to do it until the nurse came into the room to give Cindy meds. It looked to him that she'd already had a great deal of meds in her, but again, he didn't know what was going on with her.

It took them two hours to get the room cleaned up — there had been dirty linens in the corner that looked to them as if they'd been there for several days. Then, while she was given a shower — a very much needed one, as it turned out, her bed was changed, and clean sheets were put on it. When she came back from the bathroom, she looked like she had when she'd been free, only with a great deal of weight loss.

"You're not feeding her well, are you?" The doctor told Cass that her sister wasn't cooperating with them and made a mess. "Tough shit. You'll start feeding her better, or I'll have the board in here so quickly that you'll not know what hit you. How do you think someone is going to like knowing that their loved ones are being treated like this?"

"They don't care so long as they're not with them." He was sort of sad to think that might be true. "If you make a fuss about stuff, it's only going to make it harder on her when you leave. This is a state-funded facility, and we don't have the money nor the resources to help everyone that comes through those doors."

"You'll do your job, or you'll be out of one." Cass was on a roll, and he pitied the people who didn't hop to it when she wanted answers. By the time they were ready to talk to Cindy, she'd had her nails cleaned up, her hair brushed, and her room cleaned up. It certainly smelled better once they got the other linens out of the corner. They were even given chairs to sit in when they were ready to talk to her. "Cynthia, I've come to talk to you."

She was too stoned out of her mind to understand anything that was being said to her. The doctor, when he finally showed up, said it was the best way to have her, or she'd be throwing food at people and cursing. So their solution was to keep her drugged up all the time so they'd not have to deal with her. It had merit, but he still didn't like it.

He didn't like Cindy at all, but that didn't mean that he would tolerate her being treated the way that she was. Instead of sitting there being pissed off, he decided to contact his good friend and ask Brew if there was anything that could be done about this place.

"Let me check into a couple of things. I know at one time I owned one of those buildings, but I can't remember off the top of my head." When he got back to him, he was about as pissed off as he was. *"I own that place. You're saying that they're telling you it's state runned? It's not. I donated millions of dollars to that place to have it run top-notch. I don't even have a board that I answer to. My mother was in one of those when she was alive, and I, like you, was*

disgusted when I went to visit her. I'll make some calls right now."

"*Thank you. We're here with Cass's sister, and it took them two hours to make sure that she had on a clean gown and the linens changed on her bed."* He told him what he'd been told, too. *"I don't like the woman, but I don't want to see anyone treated like this. This is worse than my nightmares could have dreamed up. The staff was having a little party when we walked in this morning, and I found out it was one of the resident's birthdays. But there wasn't any of them around to have any of the cake and ice cream that was set up. I'm telling you right now, Brew, I'd be hard-pressed not to come in here as my wolf and kill all the staff off."*

"*Don't do that. We'll call that plan 'b.' I'll make a couple of more calls and see what I can do about it. Oh, you've no idea how pissed off my Calla Lily is right now. She'll be getting that viper's nest taken care of in no time."* He was glad to hear that and told his best friend that. "*She'd make a great vampire. I'm going to talk to her about a few things here, and you should see some changes soon. Oh my, tell your Cass how sorry I am that it got to this point and nothing has been done about it. I swear on the heart of my mate that it will be changed. Vipers."*

"*Thank you, Brew. You've no idea how much I appreciate this. As I said, I don't like the woman, but she's not the only one here that is being neglected."* He looked at

Cass and realized that he might have missed something while talking to Brew. Telling her what was going on so that no one could hear them talking, she smiled at him.

"I figured that you were taking care of things here. We might as well go. She's not able to function right now, and I don't like it here. Let's go get some lunch and watch what happens here from across the street. There was a nice soup and sandwich place there." He told her that he loved the way that her mind worked.

As they were leaving, he could see the head guy. They'd never caught his name on the phone. He was saying *'yes, ma'am'* a great deal, so he figured that Calla had gotten things rolling here. As they were badged out of the building, he could hear sirens coming up the street, and when they pulled in front of the place, he had to smile. Christ, this was going to be so much fun to have a front-row seat to.

People were being escorted out by the police at one point. As many as a dozen. They looked like they were the cafeteria crew and some of the nursing staff. The doctor that they had spoken to was then taken out in cuffs and chains. They both speculated what had happened to the older man when he tried to run from the police at one point. The place was gathering quite a crowd of lookee Lou's, and they both thought that it was the funniest thing ever. He only wished that he'd remembered to record things for Brew when he saw the big vampire standing in the crowd with a lot of news reporters.

Brew didn't join them before they left, and he figured that the man had enough on his mind right now and left him to it. There were other people going into the building now, and they were dressed in nurses' uniforms as well as some of them looked like cooks. It would be just like Brew to be able to get an entire crew in place with the snap of his fingers. The man was that wealthy and that powerful. By tomorrow, he'd bet that it was as if nothing happened, and the people, the residents, would be getting good care and better food than they'd had since being put into the place.

~*~

Cass sat by the headstone that had only just been put in and decided that she could talk to her dad any place that she wanted, but here offered her the most peace. There were still bunches of flowers all over his grave, and she got down on the ground and straightened them up so they looked better. Once she was done, he dusted off the top of his headstone that had her mom on it, too, for when she passed and smiled.

"You'd be so upset about all the fanfare that went on when you had your services. Flowers and condolences came from all over the world at your passing, and people are still leaving flowers at the funeral home that couldn't be collected in time." She brushed away a tear that had formed and looked around the cemetery. "You're in such a lovely place, Dad. I know you picked it out for Mom, and she loves it as well. The big tree will keep you shaded in the hotter months and cover you with leaves in the fall. I remembered how much you liked to rake the leaves up when you had time. It's beautiful out here."

She saw a couple going to what looked to her like a gravesite for a child. It broke her heart that there were so many little children's graves not far from where she was sitting. Perhaps her dad would enjoy talking to the little ones. She had to believe that there was a place that people went to when they passed on. Otherwise, her dad would just be gone like her mother someday.

"Conri is a little overwhelmed about the land that you left him. He keeps asking Howie if he wants it. It'll make a great pack land for the pack that is growing now, thanks to the king of their kind telling people what a forward-thinking alpha he is. Me too, but I don't do as much for the pack as he does. I'm the one that makes sure he has all his appointments in order." She laughed a little at that. "He had so many meetings in the day I was surprised that he ever got anything done. Now he has them once a week and he's sleeping better because he's not so stressed about them anymore."

There were loud voices at the child's headstone. The man stormed off and left the woman there. It wasn't until then that she noticed that the woman was going to have a baby. She wished her better luck with this one. Not knowing what had happened, it was all she could do for now.

"I went to see Cindy. Conri said you were calling her that, so I am, as well. But we went to see her last week, and you'd not believe the state that she was in." She told him about the visit, how she was dirty, and that people weren't taking care of the residents. "It was awful, Dad. You'd not believe how nasty the place was. But Conri called his friend the vampire and told him what was going on, and now I guess it's in perfect working order. Even Cindy is getting better care. I know that you'd want that for her. Even for all that she did to us, she's still family, and I couldn't stand to have her looking like a homeless person and not being taken care of."

The man came back with flowers, and he handed them to the woman. She hugged him, but the man just stood there. She didn't know what was going on, but she felt sorry for the two of them.

"I wonder if they'll make it. I know that I will." She plucked one of the flowers from the stem and held it up to her nose. The smell was heady, and she loved it. It reminded her of home when she lived there and the flowers that were forever in the front hall when she came home. "Conri and I are going to try for a baby the next time I'm in heat. It's a terrible name for me ovulating, but that's what they call it. Once I'm going to have our baby, I'm going to name him after you if it's a boy. Conri Howard Valley. Conri loves that name. And if we have a little girl, I'm going to name her after his and my mom. She'll be Elizabeth Ethel Valley. I love that name. It's so old-fashioned, don't you think?"

She remembered her list and pulled it out now to tell her dad what she'd been up to. When she was about halfway through the list, she remembered something else. Something about her big brother.

"Howie is dating again. No one special just yet, but he's giving it a try. He's seeing someone from the pack, and they seem to be getting along well. They're not mates, her mate died some time ago, and she has three children. You should see Howie, Dad. He just dotes on those little ones like they're his own. And he tells them about you too how you would have taken them to get ice cream daily just so they could be happy. He does it too, just so you know." She laughed a little. "He's bought him another house. It's not nearly as big as the one he shared with Margaret, but it's lovely. He's been planting flowers in the front yard since he moved in. I actually think that he was planting them even before he unpacked the first box."

Looking at her list again, she thought of Kendrick and how he'd been avoiding her lately. "I think he is thinking that I will blame him for you passing the way that you did. I don't. You left this world just the way that you wanted to, and I couldn't be happier. Mom is, too, by the way. Happy, I mean. It's only been a few weeks since you passed, but she's doing well. I think her being with you when you passed is what's giving her the strength to go on. I'm very proud of her."

She told him how she was learning to make jelly from Ethel, Conri's mom. How she'd been at pack meetings with the women and was learning too how to cook for hundreds of people. Smiling sadly, she thought of her dad and how much he was missing right now, but she couldn't be sad, she told herself. He was in a better place.

As she was sitting there, looking around the cemetery, a butterfly came and sat on her leg. The large monarch seemed to understand how special and beautiful he was and stayed on her leg for twenty minutes or longer. It was then that she remembered her dad and her on a walk in a garden once and him pointing out all the butterflies and bugs that they found on their trip. She knew it was a sign from her dad telling her that she was all right and would be from now on.

"Thank you so much, Dad. I love you." Tears streamed down her face as the butterfly landed on the headstone by her father's name. "I miss you so much, Dad, I can barely function at times. But then something like this happens, and I'm all right again. Thank you, and I love you very much."

Walking to her car, she took a small glance at the couple again. They weren't arguing anymore, but she could tell that the man was upset. He was stiff in his shoulders, and his face looked pinched. The woman was crying, sitting on the ground next to the child's marker.

Since she didn't know what was going on, she gave them a wide berth and went on her way. Whatever their problems were, she hoped they worked them out soon. A baby wouldn't fix everything, so she hoped that they understood that. Getting in her car, she sat there for several minutes as she gathered her thoughts. She needed to go home; she had plenty to do, but she always felt so rested when she left here after talking to her dad for a few minutes.

Putting her list in the glove box with the other two she'd brought out here, she was on her way home. She didn't know why she was saving the lists, but she did, and someday, she'd get them out and reread them and think of the time that she spent with her father. It was good for her to be able to do this.

Conri met her at the door when she got home. Smiling at him, he kissed her on the mouth. Asking him what that was for, he told her that he simply loved her and wanted to show her every time he saw her. Such a goof, he was, but she loved him anyway.

They spent the afternoon together going over reports from the pack. She was getting better at finding things on the report for the foodstuffs that they had stored away, and he was a great teacher, telling her what they should and should not have in their larders. It was for emergencies, and so far this month, they'd used up a good portion of it for when there was a house fire in one of the smaller homes.

"Once a year, we'll clean out the foodstuffs and use it for giveaways. There are a lot of families that show up for it, and it all goes to good places." She asked him why they stored the food at all. It seemed silly when there was a store not too far away. "I thought about that too, but there are times when we use it for making up dinners for someone who has had a loss in their family. That way, no one is out a bunch of money for food. Also, we store things like vouchers and gift cards in there."

"I don't like that at all. Something could happen to them if there was a fire. But it's better than having them in the house where we could be robbed. I guess you can think up a better place for them so that we're not taking the chance of them being destroyed."

"I'll give it some thought. I'm assuming that they're in fireproof containers." He said that they were. "Good. At least, that's something. Maybe we can put them in the bank in a safety deposit drawer or something. No, that won't work. We won't be able to get to them on the weekends or after five. I think you have the best solution for them."

They also made up a menu for the next pack meeting. And a list of those that would have to mow the area off when it was closer to the meetings. The last group that had done it did a shitty job, and Conri had to take them to task. It was good to see him not cutting them any slack when it came to doing things for the pack. But it was a lovely ceremony. She got to meet so many of the pack that night.

She's been really nervous about the meeting. But she had all of the brothers there with her, and Conri, so she needed not to worry so much. Her mom had been invited as they were going to talk about the next meeting being on the new land, but she wasn't ready to face that many people at one time. She didn't blame her; there were over four hundred pack members at those things, and it was a little scary for her to know that they could all change into wolves whenever they wished. None of them would hurt her, of course, but she was still a little nervous.

"There are some things being delivered on Thursday. Are you going to be around the house?" She told Conri that she didn't have any plans that would take her away. "Good. I need someone to sign for them. They're new computers for the pack house. I guess the kids at the schools need a place where they can get on the internet and rather than buying a lot of computers for everyone that needs one, I thought that we could put them in the pack house for everyone to use. It certainly would make it easier for them to be used there instead of in the houses."

"I like that idea. How many did you get?" He told her that he'd gotten ten computers and three printers. "That's wonderful. You're such a brilliant man."

"I feel like you're buttering me up for something. Or did I do something that you need to talk to me about?" She told him not to be so paranoid that she was just complimenting him. "You can butter me up when you want something. I'd give it to you anyway because I love you that much, but I'd love to be able to figure out what I've done so that I can worry a little. You make it too easy to be your mate when you're so agreeable all the time."

"I don't want to fight with you. It's nice just having you around all the time. I especially like that

I can talk to you whenever I like. You make me feel good." He told her that it was his pleasure. "Thank you for that. I have some things that I need to get done if I'm going to be home for supper. There are two meetings that the pack women are having that they want me there for. I think they invite me because they're afraid of you. But I don't mind all that much. It's nice of them to have me around too. One is about the food for the next meeting and the second one is about daycare for the little ones. Did you know that the older generation watches over the little ones two days a week to help out the mothers? It's nice they said because they can teach the kids the old ways and stories and the moms can get their house cleaned up for a few minutes before the kids mess it up again."

"I think that I did know that but forgot about it. You'll learn that they can't do much without asking you or me for permission. It's not always needed, but they ask me all the same. They'll ask you now, too. Just go with your gut on some of the things, and it'll work out." She said she'd have to remember that. "All right. Be on your way, and I will, too, or we'll end up in bed again. Not that I don't love having you there all the time, but I'm getting behind on my work chasing you around the house. Go now before I change my mind."

She was still laughing when she went out the door to her car. They had been spending a great deal of time in the bed, the kitchen, and the dining room. Anywhere there was a sturdy surface, they'd make love several times a day that way. It was exhilarating and relaxing at the same time.

Chapter 10

Kendrick locked up his house and made his way to the car. He was closed up today and had plans that were going to take him out of town. At least, that was his plan right now. He could barely go anywhere without someone asking him what a mark was on their hand or if they needed stitches in a cut. Being a doctor had its ups and downs, but today, he was going to be out of his doctor wardrobe and into fun clothing.

"Hey, Doc Kendrick? Whatcha doing today?" He told the little Shaver boy that he was going out of town. "Who you got covering for you? Momma said you're the only thing that keeps us kids from the hospital all the time."

"I don't need anyone to cover for me, Sammie. I'm going to have myself an adventure today." He looked at him strangely. "You'll be fine for a few hours, but do me a favor, don't get into trouble while I'm gone. You'll have to hold off on your own adventures today."

"That'll be hard to do. I like adventures." He got into his car before the little bugger hurt himself and delayed his trip. He was still standing in the street when he pulled onto Main Street to get out of town.

Stopping to get gas, he hurried through the process and paid. He didn't want to be caught now that he was almost out of town. As soon as he was back in his car, his brother reached out to him.

"Whatever it is, I don't want to deal with it. It's my first trip out of town in a couple of years. I kid you not, I'm going out of town today and find something that interests me." Conri laughed. "It's not funny. I'm serious here. I need some me time, or I'm going to quit being a doctor and become a monk or something."

"I was going to invite you to hang out with Cass and me. We're going to go to the flea market in Rainersville today. They had all kinds of fair food we're going to have." He asked when they were leaving. "We're leaving the house now. Why don't we meet up in the little town and drive together to the market? It'll be fun."

"I'll do it. But I'm not taking my cell phone in. I'm off today, and I have my service directing everyone to call 911 if they need assistance that bad." He told him it was a good idea. "I'll meet you at the gas station right inside of town."

It was an hour's drive from Dresden to Rainersville, but it usually was well worth it. They had sales on everything from ducks and rabbits to guns and ammo. And everything in between. The last time he was there, he'd gotten some really good deep-fried pork rings. And he'd been able to pick up some really nice flowering baskets for his front porch. Now that he had a destination in mind, he was about as excited as he'd been when he left his house this morning.

Pulling into the gas station, he filled up his car and got permission to leave it on the lot, out of the way, so that he could ride with his brother and Cass. Getting him a couple of bottles of water, the humidity of the day making him doubly thirsty, he drank the first one down too quickly and felt a little off. Careful of the second one, he watched as the people got their gas and sodas while in the little convenience store that was in every small town across the state.

Conri pulled in about twenty minutes after he did. By that time, he was finished with his second bottle of water and needed to use the restroom. While they got drinks to take the edge off, Cass said, he went to the bathroom and washed up his face. He was still excited about his day but was being careful of the heat and humidity of the day. A person could get really sick on days like today if they didn't take care of themselves.

The first half hour, they walked around the booths. People were selling all kinds of junk—to him, anyway. But there were some nice treasures in among the things that they were selling. He found a nice knife that he could carry around for five bucks. There were tools galore that you could pick up for less than ten bucks. He found L.E.D. lights that he got so that he could line his kids' office. They would change colors with just a twist of a dial that came with it. Then they got to the trees that shaded the animals for sale. Mostly, it was chickens and hunting dogs that were under the trees, but there were other things as well.

Someone was selling eggs. There were also rabbits and ducks. He wanted some ducks for his pond on his land, but he didn't want to purchase them here and have to lug them all the way back home in his car. And guns. There were so many young people carrying guns that he noticed that they were far more careful with them than they were keeping an eye on their children.

When they decided to have lunch, he knew just what he was getting. A bucket of fries and a hamburger to go with it. There were so many fries in his bucket that he was glad to share them with his family. Then, the fire department for the area was having a bake sale, so he got him some cookies to go with it for dessert. The lemon shake he got hit the spot better than anything else he'd been drinking along the lanes of tents and caravans put up.

"I'm getting me some of the leather straps that the guy over there is selling. I'm going to use them to hang up things in the yard. He said they were durable." Conri told Cass that they would dry out in the weather and the things would fall to the ground. "Oh. He didn't say that part. Mean old man." Then she laughed. "I'm going to get them anyway. I can use them for one season and come back next year for some more of them."

The only thing that he'd bought so far was drinks, and he'd gotten a lot of those. He knew better than to be dehydrated in this kind of setting and was making sure he didn't get sunstroke. He was also making sure that Cass and Conri didn't either. Encouraging them to stand in the shade when they could and to drink as much as they could.

He enjoyed the rest of his afternoon, and when they were ready to call it quits, he was ready as well. Going to two of the booths that he'd wanted to get some flowers from, he was able to get a better deal because it was the end of the weekend for most of the people here. He got his flowers at both booths for half price and picked up some planters too that he was going to fill with fall cabbage, too. It was turning out to be a better day than he'd thought he'd have today when he left home.

Getting back to the gas station where he'd left his car, still there, thankfully, he put his purchases in the back of his car and went into the store to thank the woman who had let him park there. As soon as he was in the line, he knew something was going on. He could smell blood. And lots of it.

"She's cut herself on the slicer." The elderly woman was ringing out people while covered in blood. "I've called an ambulance, but they're having trouble getting through the traffic."

"I can help. I'm a doctor. I'll just go get my bag." He ran out to his car to get his bag and was back in the store in seconds. His brother had already left, so he didn't need to stop and talk to him. He found the young girl in the back room holding paper towels over a good-sized slice in her hand. He asked her what she'd done.

"I was slicing meat when the turkey fell over, and I reached up before I could think that was a bad idea and adjusted the loaf. The slicer didn't care that I wasn't part of the turkey and sliced me through my hand. Am I gonna die from loss of blood?" He told her that he'd take care of her. "Good. I have a blind date tonight, and I didn't want to go. Don't you hate it when people set you up for a date when all you want to do is read a good book and go to bed early? If not, then I must be an odd woman out."

"I'd rather read a book too. I don't even care if it's a terrible book so long as I don't have to go out with a stranger when people are thinking that we're getting married. Can you please hold your hand still? I'm going to stitch it up loosely to make sure that the blood stops flowing."

He didn't stitch it tightly but only closed the four-inch wound. They'd have to clean it out when she got to the hospital, and he didn't want to put her through that twice. As soon as the ambulance showed up, he told them what he'd done and how she'd been reacting when they asked. He was asked if he could go to the hospital with her, and he said that he didn't have any privileges at the local hospital here.

"We would like you to go in case someone has questions at the other end. Even if you could follow us in your car, that would be a great help to the doctors at the clinic in the event that they need you to answer things that we might not know." He couldn't help but feel like he was being bamboozled into going but ended up following the ambulance with a cruiser behind him to keep him out of trouble for following at the speed they were going. He really wanted to go home and read a crappy book over this.

It took another hour to get to the hospital in their town. He wondered how they were able to keep others from dying with it seemingly far away and the traffic being as bad as it was. When they pulled into the emergency department, he parked his car in the lanes, too, and went inside. He didn't figure he'd be there very long if he was only answering questions for the people inside.

He should have known better.

After several hours in the department, helping treat others who had been brought in from the market days, he was ready to get a hotel and sleep it off before trying to get home. He was beyond exhausted, and he knew that his car was going to be towed as no one would allow him to go out and move it. The young woman that he'd come in with had been released hours ago after getting fifty-four stitches in her hand and sent home.

At three-thirty in the morning, he was given a room with a cot where he could sleep it off. Exhausted, he didn't even care that the bed was hard as stone and the sheets were too small for his large frame. Almost as soon as he laid his head down, he was out. It had been a terribly long day, and he was glad that it was over.

~*~

Sharon didn't know what to do about her hand and getting out of work. She'd been able to get out of the blind date, thankfully, and now she had to figure out how she was going to go to her job while being bandaged up like she was.

"You can run the register." She supposed that she could expect to bag things up. "You'll be fine. I can do the rest, and we just won't have any sammiches for the day. I'll have one of the others come in and slice meat up, and I'll make them in between customers if it comes to that. You got yourself some pain pills, don't you?"

"I do, but they make me woozy a little bit." Daff, an apt name if she'd ever heard one, said that she'd make sure that she was up on her feet. "I just don't want to cause you any more trouble than I already have."

"This is my shop, and I do what I want. You don't have to do anything with the people getting gas, so that's gonna be all right. You just ring them out, and we'll have a productive day today." She said she'd try not to do too much that would cause her double work. "You just be you, honey. You'll see that people can be kind when they wanna. I know a few people around here that sets stock in you."

She had no idea what that meant but let it go. Sometimes, having Daff explain something was worse than having her just say it and move on. So here she was, running the register in the busiest part of the day, hoping to goodness that she could get a break soon so she could pee. Another hard job when you only had one hand to adjust and pull up your pants.

"Should you be working?" She'd heard that at least a dozen times today and always just nodded and said she was fine. Daff was doing a good job of keeping her from using her hand a great deal. When someone came into the shop, and they had pops and more stuff than they could carry, she'd have them bagged up and out the door sometimes before they got their change.

By lunch, she'd had enough and only wanted to sit down and have a break with a pain pill. Taking half of one was almost as bad as taking a whole one, but it did take the pain away for a little while. Coming out of the back room, she saw the doctor who had helped her last night.

"I wanted to check on you and see how you were doing? Should you be here?" She explained to him how she wasn't doing anything but running the register for the place and that Daff had the rest under control. "I did notice last night that she seems to know what she's doing. Today, I'm headed home. I was at the hospital until all hours last night, and all I want to do is check on you and make sure you're all right, then head home."

"I'm sure that the hospital was happy for your help. I know that I was when you came in." She thought the man was about as handsome as she'd ever met. Even as tired as he looked, he looked good enough to snack on. Embarrassed, she changed the subject. "My hand doesn't hurt too badly right now. I know that they had to put in a lot of stitches in it, and I'm grateful for what you did for me."

"It wasn't anything. Just getting the wound closed so that you'd stop bleeding was first and foremost. Then, once you were at the hospital, they got it cleaned up and sealed for you. You're lucky you didn't lose a finger. I hope you're more careful next time." She thought that he looked embarrassed and smiled a little. "Anyway, I just wanted to check on you and see how you're doing."

He looked hesitant to leave. She didn't mind him hanging around, so when the next customer came in, she dealt with him and the next two afterwards. She was ringing out the next customer when he suddenly asked her if she'd like to have dinner with him.

"I mean, I know that we can't go to a steak house. You'd be hard-pressed to cut up yours, but I could do it. It won't be like a blind date for us since we know one another. Sort of. I'm Kendrick Valley. I'm a medical doctor for Dresden and the local hospital. And you're Sharon." She told him her last name. "Sharon Taylor. It's lovely to meet you."

"Same from me." She felt silly again and rang out a couple more people. "I'd love to have any kind of dinner with you. And you're right. It wouldn't be like a blind date. Besides, I don't have any bad books I can read at the moment." They both laughed.

"Would tonight be all right with you? I'd understand if you just wanted to go home and rest your hand with some pain medication. We can do it some other night this week." She said that she really was all right and wanted to have dinner with him. "I have a better idea. How about I pick up some pizza tonight, and then we can have dinner together on Friday night. That should be better for your hand and me getting a good day's sleep in. I'll call you too. If that's all right?"

"It would be perfect. I love pizza." She really did, too, and was glad that he suggested it so that she could rest her hand, too. It really wasn't as great feeling as she said it was, and she was sure that he knew it. "I'll write down my address for you, and since you don't know the pizza places around here, I'll order one for us so that we can get to know one another. What do you think of that?"

"Perfect." She gave him her address and a time. She'd order the pizza and make sure that it was delivered on time. When he reached for the piece of paper, their hands brushed one another, and she felt a tingling that she'd never experienced before. It was like a connection or something. After he left her. She did wonder what he was going to do for the rest of the day while he waited around for her to get off work.

~*~

Kendrick knew that she was his mate but wasn't at all sure how to go about telling her that he was a wolf and that she was his other half. He didn't even know if she knew what a shifter was. She hadn't smelled like anyone that could shift had been around her, but then she had been covered in a good amount of blood, and that could have been it. It had taken him at least two hours to figure out why he kept getting drawn back to the area that she'd been in, and then it hit him. She was his mate. Kendrick thought about what his brother would say if he were to tell him.

They'd make fun of him is what would happen. They were relentless in their teasing of Conri, and he was their alpha. They'd be terrible with him if they found out, and he just didn't want to hear it. Not until he got to know her better, anyway. Besides, he might well be mistaken.

"Nah, she's the one. You knew it last night and then today, moron." He put gas in his car and paid at the pump so as not to get in her hair again. But damn, but he wanted to. He felt the need to heal her, too. To make her pain, which was pushing at him, to make go away, too. "I'll tell her tonight when I see her. I'll just set her down and tell her that I'm a wolf shifter and that I'm mated to her. That should be good."

It wasn't good that he was talking to himself again. He only did that when he was nervous, and he was very nervous right now. Going back to the hotel that he'd rented this morning, he decided to go and find a place where he could get him some jeans and some other things to change into. He didn't want to smell like blood, which he could smell on himself when having a date with his other half. He kept telling himself that. That he'd seen and met his other half and would spend the rest of his life with her.

He found a Walmart not far from where he was staying. Getting himself some jeans and other things that he was going to need, he put them all in a cart and made his way to the front of the store. He thought about getting a case of water, he did need one at home, but he thought about dragging it all the way back with him and decided that he'd get it later. Right now, it was up in the air when he was going to be going back home. He had a practice, sure, but he'd cleaned the next two days for himself so that he could get to know Sharon.

While in line, he found himself a book. It was one that he'd not read yet, and he tossed it into his cart. He had lots of time to waste between now and five-thirty and didn't want to seem like a stocker by hanging around at the gas station. He didn't want to scare her off before he'd even gotten to meet her.

Going back to the hotel, he took a long hot shower and changed into his new clothing. Shaving, too, he felt at least a little better about going out now and sat down on his bed to start on his book. It was hard for him to get into it because he kept thinking that he was going to forget the time, and he finally set an alarm. Fat lot of good it had done him.

He kept making sure that he'd set the alarm right. When that was correct, he had to make sure that his phone was charged up and wouldn't die when he needed it to remind him when to go. Christ, this was worse than when he was studying for his exams. He'd been checking on things so much that he nearly overslept when he finally fell asleep in his dorm room.

At some point, he fell asleep and was awakened by the alarm that he had set correctly. Getting up and brushing his teeth and combing his hair, he was ready to leave when his cell phone rang. It was Sharon. Sitting down, just knowing that she was going to cancel, he answered the phone with his name.

"It's Sharon. Sharon Taylor. I wanted to let you know that the pizza isn't going to be delivered because they're short-staffed at the moment, and I wondered if you could pick it up on your way to my house." He said that he could do that and wrote down the address. "They said it would be all right if you picked it up and that I ordered it. The people there know that I order all the time and were worried that I was getting myself into something bad. So if they give you the fifth degree, that's why. They're slightly overly protective of me."

"Good. You need to have someone watch over you sometimes. Right?" She said she supposed so and told him she'd see him in a little while. Just before she hung up, she asked him if he liked beer or tea with his pizza. "Both, but I'll stick to tea with you. You don't want to be drinking with those pain pills they gave you."

"It's funny, but after seeing you today, I've not had a bit of pain today. It's like it's all healed up." He'd not thought of that him touching her might do that. "All right, I'll see you soon. I'm really looking forward to this tonight."

"So am I. I'll see you soon, Sharon." Leaving the hotel, he was on his way to the pizza place in a few minutes. As soon as he arrived and told them who he was picking up for, they did ask him a lot of questions. They didn't seem impressed with him being a doctor because, of course, doctors could be predators, too.

"I know your name now, so you'd be better off behaving yourself. I like Sharon, and she's a good girl. A little on the shy side, but she's a good girl to everyone." He promised the owner of the pizza place that he'd be on his best behavior. "See that you do. I'm not opposed to killing you if you hurt her."

"I'd allow you to do that too if I were to harm a hair on her head. She means a great deal to me as well." One of the others whispered in his ear, and the boss looked at him. Then he leaned over the counter and asked him if he was a wolf. "I am. And if you know that, you know that as my mate, I won't harm her at all. I'm going to talk to her tonight about it."

He nodded before speaking again. "You see that you do. And I don't want to hear about you taking advantage of her just because she's your mate, either. I know that it's rare, but you behave yourself too. Like I said, she's a good girl."

"I promise you on the heart of my mother she'll be as safe with me as she would be with you." That seemed to satisfy him, and he handed over the pizza. "Call it a pre-wedding gift for the two of you. Now get on out of here before it gets cold. Pizza…my pizza isn't good cold. You eat it hot or not at all."

"Thank you." He didn't even feel jealous about the man drilling him about Sharon. He was glad that someone was out there watching over her for him. And when he got to the house, he was very glad when she asked who it was before opening the door to him. Yes, she was going to be safe with him forever.

"This is the best pizza, wouldn't you agree?" He said that he'd never had one better. I never thought to ask you if you'd like a meat one. But then, I guess you eat a great deal of meat." He asked her what she meant. "Grizzle called here after you left the pizza shop. He told me to have an open mind and that you were a shifter. A wolf shifter. And that you had something to talk to me about. Is that all true?"

"It is. And since I'm assuming you're not flying off the handle or anything, you know what you are to me." She nodded and suddenly found her pants interesting. "Look at me, Sharon. I won't ever hurt you. Not in any way."

"I know that. I don't know why I know that, but I do. Also, you healed my hand for me, didn't you?" He said that he didn't know. He'd never had a mate before and didn't know what he could do with just a touch. "It doesn't hurt at all. I've been tempted to pull the bandages off and look for myself, but I'm afraid of what I might see. Is that something that mates are supposed to be able to do to each other?"

"I don't know, honestly. What I do know was that today, when you passed me the note with your address on it, I felt something tingle. Did you feel anything?" She told him that she'd felt the same thing. "Then I can only assume. If it's not healed up, I can put the bandages back on you. I never go without my medical bag. I even filled it out today when I was at the store. I'm always afraid of not having what I need the next time, so I always do that when I'm…I'm babbling. I want to see it, too."

She undid the wrap and, with shaking hands, showed him what was left of her wound. Just black threads in the wrapping and nothing more. Even the cut looked healed. The scar was still pink, but it was about as good-looking as if it had happened months ago instead of last night. He kissed the area, and she inhaled sharply.

"You're beautiful, Sharon." She slid to the floor with him, and he kissed her again. This time on the mouth. "You're so very beautiful that I'm excited for the next thousand years or so hanging out with you."

"That's a long time." He'd tell her later that they had that much and more to be together. Tonight was for them. "I'm not much of a catch, I'm afraid. Daff was allowing me to work so that I could have some income. She's good to me."

"You won't have to worry about money again, love. I have enough for us." She nodded, and he smiled. "Can I kiss you again? You taste like pizza and beer, and that's so good."

He had to calm his wolf a couple of times when they got into kissing heavily. As soon as she got up to clean up their mess, he had a good talk with himself and his wolf. He didn't want to make love to her on the night he promised to behave himself. No, he was going to be a good man and woo her first.

"I have some dessert. I have apple pie and lemon refrigerator cake. Which do you want?" Two of his favorites, how was he to choose? It was going to be difficult being a good man with a woman who spoke to his inner beast.

Before You Go...

HELP AN AUTHOR

write a review

THANK YOU!

Share your voice and help guide other readers to these wonderful books. Even if it's only a line or two, your reviews help readers discover the author's books so they can continue creating stories that you'll love. Log in to your favorite retailer and leave a review. Thank you.

AWARD WINNING, BESTSELLING AUTHOR

Kathi Barton, a winner of the Pinnacle Book Achievement Award and a best-selling author on Amazon and All Romance books, lives in Nashport, Ohio, with her husband, Paul. When not creating new worlds and romance, Kathi and her husband enjoy camping and going to auctions. She can also be seen at county fairs with her husband, an artist, and potter.

Her muse, a cross between Jimmy Stewart and Hugh Jackman, brings her stories to life for her readers in a way that has them coming back time and again for more. Her favorite genre is paranormal romance, with a great deal of spice. You can visit Kathi online and drop her an email if you'd like. She loves hearing from her fans. aaronskiss@gmail.com.

Follow Kathi on her blog: http://kathisbartonauthor.blogspot.com/

www.ingramcontent.com/pod-product-compliance
Lightning Source LLC
Chambersburg PA
CBHW032000170626
46807CB00006B/2577